Forgiving Moses

ROOSEVELT HIGH SCHOOL SERIES

Forgiving Moses

ROOSEVELT HIGH SCHOOL SERIES

Gloria L. Velásquez

PIÑATA BOOKS
ARTE PÚBLICO PRESS
HOUSTON, TEXAS

Forgiving Moses is made possible through a grant from the City of Houston through the Houston Arts Alliance. We are grateful for their support.

Piñata Books are full of surprises!

Piñata Books
An imprint of
Arte Público Press
University of Houston
4902 Gulf Fwy, Bldg 19, Rm 100
Houston, Texas 77204-2004

Cover illustration by Anne Vega
Cover design by Robert Vega

Names: Velásquez, Gloria, author.
Title: Forgiving Moses / by Gloria L. Velásquez.
Description: Houston, TX : Piñata Books, an imprint of Arte Público Press, [2018] | Summary: At his fourth school in four years, Moses Vargas explodes when it is revealed that his father is in prison, but in a support group for teens with absentee fathers, he begins finding better ways to cope. Includes glossary.
Identifiers: LCCN 2017061338 (print) | LCCN 2018007957 (ebook) | ISBN 9781518504990 (epub) | ISBN 9781518505003 (kindle) | ISBN 9781518505010 (pdf) | ISBN 9781558858640 (alk. paper)
Subjects: | CYAC: Prisoners' families—Fiction. | Fathers and sons—Fiction. | Family problems—Fiction. | High schools—Fiction. | Schools—Fiction. | Mexican Americans—Fiction.
Classification: LCC PZ7.V488 (ebook) | LCC PZ7.V488 Fo 2018 (print) | DDC [Fic]—dc23
LC record available at https://lccn.loc.gov/2017061338

Printed in the United States of America
Cushing-Malloy, Inc., Ann Arbor, MI
May 2018–June 2018
7 6 5 4 3 2 1

IN LOVING MEMORY

OF

JUAN RICARDO LOPEZ

Mi gran amor eterno
1958–2014

ONE
Moses

I'm dreaming I'm back in Salinas when I'm suddenly jolted into the present. "Mom says it's time to get up," my little sister, Carmen, hollers out. I wait for a moment until I hear the door shut and I know she's gone. I roll onto my back, trying hard to retrieve images from my dream. I was with my best friend, Arturo, and we were washing his Mom's blue Honda. Even though it was an old car with huge dents in it, Arturo's mom used to give him twenty bucks every time he washed it. I'd usually go over to help, and when we were done we'd go to Dominic's and stuff our faces with pizza. How I wish I were back in Salinas with Arturo instead of here in this strange apartment in a foreign city.

As I slide out of bed and reach for my jeans, I imagine that I'm going to meet Arturo at the bus stop like I did every morning. Arturo wouldn't stop talking while we waited for the bus that would take us to Salinas High. And almost every conversation was about girls and cars. I used to tease him about which was better—the girl or the car, and he'd laugh saying, "Hey, bro, can't have one without the other."

It makes me sick to think of another new school. This is my fourth school since junior high. First, we moved to Tehachapi, then Delano, then Salinas. And now . . . this dumb ass place, only this one is worse. Why can't we just stay in one city? I'm sick of it all. It's so depressing. New teachers. New schedules. New friends. Seems like just when I make a good friend like Arturo, we move again. Why can't it all stay the same for once?

I can smell Mom's coffee as I walk into the kitchen. Mom is sitting at the table with Carmen, who is having some Rice Krispies. Mom is dressed in her ugly, pink CNA scrubs. Her dark brown hair is pulled back with a clip, making her full face stand out even more. There are traces of blue eyeshadow on her eyelids. Mom hardly ever wears make-up except for her beige lipstick.

As I pour myself some cereal, she says, "*Hijo,* I'll drop you both off at school on my way to the nursing home."

"I'm fed up with moving around. Why couldn't we have stayed in Salinas?"

Mom shakes her head. "You know why we moved here, *hijo.* You watch, you'll make new friends in no time."

Wiggling in her chair as if she has to go to the bathroom, Carmen says, "I already made friends with Tammy. She lives in the apartment next to us. I think she has an older brother. Maybe you can meet him."

It's a good thing Carmen is only in third grade; otherwise she'd hate this as much as I do. It's all an adventure for her.

"Thanks, but no thanks," I answer, realizing Carmen is only trying to make me feel better. If only I could be that innocent and carefree. If only I didn't hate my life.

"Time to go," Mom says, lifting her small round body from the kitchen chair. "Carmen, don't forget your backpack."

Ten minutes later, we pull up to the front of César Chávez Elementary School. I wait in the car while Mom walks Carmen to her classroom. Rolling my window down for some fresh air, I can hear car doors slamming as parents drop off their kids. Gazing around at the fancy houses with perfectly trimmed lawns, all I can think about is how to start all over again. You'd think this was just another day, that I'd be used to it, but I'm not. I wonder if Arturo already found another friend to replace me. I promised I'd call him, but what for? I'd have to fake it, pretend that everything is cool.

Mom does her best to sound cheerful as she climbs back in the car and we drive away. "Isn't it pretty here?" she says, pointing to the golden rolling hills in the background as we head toward the downtown area. It almost looks like a scene from a postcard, wide tree-lined streets with beautiful mountain peaks in the background.

"I like Salinas better," I insist, remembering it's rundown buildings, bustling streets and used car lots. Arturo and I would walk around for hours checking out the cars for sale. Then we'd eat at our favorite Mexican *taquería*. I'll never forget the smell of the *carne asada* being grilled and how Don Raimundo, the owner, liked to tease us, calling us *vagos* the moment we arrived.

Mom doesn't speak again until we arrive at Roosevelt High. "It looks like a newer school," she says as we turn onto the campus packed with students and cars. It's definitely smaller and more modern compared to Salinas High, which was made up of several old, historic buildings. It almost took up an entire block. Mom is about to drive me all the way up to the front, but I stop her. "Right here's fine," I demand, so she pulls over to the side.

"*Hijo*, I know you're not happy about this, but we all have to try to make the best of it. And don't forget to go home on the bus. Carmen will be at Mrs. Pantoja's until you pick her up. I'll be home by five."

"*Make the best of it*," I mutter under my breath, slamming the door behind me. How am I supposed to do that when I feel so miserable? Reluctantly, I make my way through groups of strangers. *Mostly white kids,* I think to myself until I hear a group of students speaking in English *and* Spanish. A short girl with black, wavy hair and bright red lipstick smiles at me as I walk past them.

In the main office, I go straight to the front desk. The receptionist, who is wearing a pair of weird purple-rimmed glasses that clash with her bright red hair, greets me with a friendly smile.

"Good morning. I'm Jan. What can I help you with?" she asks in a high soprano voice that makes me want to cover my ears.

"I'm Moses Vargas. It's my first day here."

"Welcome. We're happy to have you here."

As she hands me my schedule, she tells me I will have to go talk to Mrs. Bates, the freshman counselor. I follow her around the corner to the counseling area where she points out Mrs. Bates' office.

"Thank you," I say as she wishes me good luck.

Tapping lightly on the door, I take in a deep breath. I know it's time to pretend, to suck it all up just like the last time. Moments later, a slender woman wearing a red blazer with grey slacks, opens the door and lets me in.

"We've been expecting you, Moses. Welcome to Roosevelt." Mrs. Bates shakes my hand, inviting me to take a seat on the small wooden chair next to her desk.

While she pulls up my schedule on her computer, I glance at the framed photograph of Mrs. Bates with her family. They all look so happy that I'm tempted to turn the picture face down.

"I've already seen your transcripts—you're a very good student, especially in math and science," Mrs. Bates says. "You have algebra first period, science second, English third, then lunch. In the afternoon you have P.E. and computer science. It's a good schedule since your most difficult classes are in the morning." She pauses to hand me a tardy slip, a map of the campus and a student planner. "I've also included a list of our clubs and sports in case you're interested in joining one. Do you have any questions?"

I quietly shake my head side to side.

"Well then, let me call one of our student assistants so they can walk you over to the math building."

"I can find it on my own," I insist, rising to my feet. The last thing I need is for everyone to think I'm a big baby. It's bad enough that I'm the new *tonto* on the block.

Mrs. Bates nods. "Remember, Moses. If you have any questions, come see me any time."

It only takes me a few minutes to find the math building. I'm a genius with maps. When I walk into algebra and hand the teacher the tardy slip, I feel sweat trickling down my armpits. Everyone is staring at me.

"Welcome, Moses. I'm Mr. Bukowski, better known as Mr. B." His broad face breaks into a smile, revealing several crooked teeth. "We're on page 120—please take that seat," he says, pointing to the empty desk on the third row. In a few minutes, I'm immersed in the world of algebra. I've always loved math, ever since I was in elementary. Logarithmic functions don't faze me at all. Arturo used to tease me about being a math nerd. He could barely figure out basic problems, and I used to help him all the time with his homework.

I'm almost finished with the assignment when the bell rings. I stuff my math book and binder back into my backpack, and make my way to the noisy hallway. At least my science class is in the same building and I don't have to pull out my map and search for it.

By lunchtime, I'm fed up with everyone looking at me. All I want is to be alone, so I go to the library where I find a quiet corner in the back. Ignoring my growling stomach, I pick up a *National Geographic* off the nearest table. This month's issue is about Costa Rica. The first article is about the weirdly named Bri Bri, an indigenous people on the Caribbean coast. I imagine myself wandering through the tropical forests of Costa Rica, forgetting all about being a stranger in a new city and school.

TWO
Moses

My head is throbbing by the end of fifth period, but at least my first day has ended. I can go home now, kick back, be myself and not feel as if I've contracted some sort of deadly virus that makes everyone avoid me.

When I get to the bus stop, there are already a bunch of students waiting, so I hurry to get in line.

"You're the new guy, right?" says the dude in front of me. "I'm Manuel. We live in the same apartment complex."

"Oh, yeah?" I say, staring at Manuel's handsome, brown face and wavy, black hair. I'm trying hard to remember if I saw him in one of my classes when the bus driver signals that he is about to close the door.

Following Manuel onto the crowded bus, I realize that he's several inches shorter than me. Arturo used to tease me that Mexicans were supposed to be short, not 5'8" like me. I once asked my mom about my height and she explained it came from my great-grandfather, who was a Tarahumara Indian from the Chihuahua desert in northern Mexico.

As we go down the aisle, two cute girls sitting in the third row ask Manuel to sit with them.

"Sorry, *chulas*, I'm sitting with my bro today," he says, winking at them. "

We find an empty seat at the back of the bus and as I slide onto the seat next to him, I get a strong whiff of Old Spice. "Where'd you move from?" Manuel asks.

I'm suddenly back in P.E. class with the two white students who asked me the same question only I lied and told them I was from San Francisco. After that, they wouldn't shut up about the Golden Gate Bridge and Alcatraz Island. I had to pretend I'd been there. Then, in computer science, I was forced to repeat the same story to the chatty girl sitting next to me. Although I'm tempted to lie again, Manuel's kind eyes compel me to tell him the truth.

"I'm from Salinas."

"Really?" Manuel says, smoothing out his Elvis Presley hair with a sleek, black comb. "Heard there's a lot of gangs out there."

"They don't bother you if you don't bother them."

Slipping his comb back into his shirt pocket, Manuel turns his attention toward the girl with bright red lipstick sitting in front of us and begins to flirt. Manuel is clearly the most popular guy on the bus. Watching him make his moves, I wonder what it feels like to be the center of attention and to want that.

When he turns his attention back to me, Manuel lowers his voice. "Roosevelt has the finest girls—I can hook you up any time you want." When I insist I'm fine, Manuel pats me on the back. "Okay, bro, but remember, I'm your connection."

As soon as the bus drops us off, Manuel asks if I want to hang out for a while.

"Sorry, I can't. My mom doesn't get home until five, so I have to watch my sister."

"That sucks," Manuel says. "What time does your dad get home?"

The words spill out before I can stop them. "My dad's dead."

I quickly turn around before Manuel can ask any more questions.

∽ ∽ ∽

Mrs. Pantoja lives on the floor above us. She doesn't speak any English because she just moved here from Mexico. In my broken Spanish I explain that I'm Carmen's brother. Drying her hands on her blue apron, Mrs. Pantoja smiles and shakes my hand.

Within seconds, Carmen appears at my side with a tiny girl wearing pigtails. Stuffing the last piece of her *quesadilla* in her mouth, Carmen says, "My brother's here. We can play tomorrow." The little girl looks as if she is about to cry when Carmen follows me outside to the stairway.

"Moses, can you read a book with me? We went to the library today and I checked out a book about a purple dinosaur."

If anyone can snap me out of a bad mood, it's my little sister. I playfully say, "There's no such thing as purple dinosaurs."

"Yes, there are," Carmen insists, tilting her head sideways and raising her voice.

I want to reach out and softly pull her ponytail, tell her I'm only joking, but I know it won't do any good. Carmen not only looks like Mom with those huge, brown eyes and heart-shaped face, but she's even more stubborn.

The moment I unlock the front door the phone starts to ring. When I pick it up, I'm greeted by the familiar recording: *You have a collect call from an inmate in the California Department of Corrections.*

I can feel the hair rise on the back of my neck. I hear Dad repeat his name as the recording instructs me to say "yes" or press one if I want to accept. I'm tempted to hang up, pretend it was a wrong number, but I imagine Mom's excitement every time Dad calls.

Breathing in slowly, I whisper "yes" and Dad's voice comes back on.

"Hello," I say quietly.

"Son, how are you?"

"Okay," I mumble, glancing around the room at the stained carpet, the fake, black leather couch, and the cheap Walmart end tables. The only nice thing in the room is the new television we bought two years ago when the old one finally gave out. Mom had to use her entire tax return to purchase it since Dad wasn't around to help us.

"How's your new school?"

I clench my fist. Why the hell does he even ask?

"It's fine," I answer, biting the inside of my lip until I taste blood. We don't say anything for what feels like a long time.

We're suddenly interrupted by the recorded message announcing we only have five minutes left to talk. "I know your mom's not home," Dad says, "but, can I talk with your sister?"

By now, Carmen is standing at my side. "Is that Daddy? I want to talk to him!"

As I go into the kitchen for something to drink, I hear Carmen describing her new school. If only I were nine years old again like Carmen, maybe Dad would still be my hero, someone to admire.

I'm about to take another sip, when Carmen shouts, "Hurry, Moses, Dad wants to talk to you again."

I slam my cup on the counter and head back into the living room. Dad is speaking quickly.

"Tell your mom I turned in the visiting form. She should get approved for a visit by next week. Hope you can come too."

Then I hear a click. There is dead silence. For a second I feel panic, but then I remember all the times Mom has been disconnected in the middle of a sentence.

"I wanted to say bye," Carmen says, tears forming in her eyes.

"Why don't you read me that book about the crazy dinosaur?"

A smile spreads across Carmen's face as she races off for her backpack.

An hour later, I'm sitting on my bed reading about melting glaciers for science class when Mom walks into my room.

"Carmen said your dad called. Did he say anything about the visiting form?"

Eyeing Mom closely, I am filled with pity. Her scrubs have several stains on them and her face is a wreck. She looks like she's been through hell. "He said he got it, that he already turned it in."

Mom's lips form into a smile. I know she's already counting the days until she can go see him. "That's good. Maybe we can visit this weekend. Did he say when he's calling again?"

"No. Can I please finish my homework?"

As Mom turns around to leave, I feel a tightness in my chest. Doesn't she know how much I hate being her messenger? I drop my science book to the floor and grab my binder. A Polaroid of Dad and I falls onto my lap. We were at Tehachapi. It was Father's Day. I gaze at Dad's handsome face; the perfect movie star nose, the high cheekbones, the intense dark eyes.

I remember the time I complained to Arturo about looking like my dad. He thought I was crazy. "Dude, you've got it made—the girls are always flirting with you!"

I quickly stuff the photograph back into my binder, wondering why God had to curse me like this. Why the hell can't I look more like Mom?

THREE
Moses

By the time I walk into first period Algebra I feel as if I've already made some new friends. On the bus this morning, Manuel not only saved a seat for me, but he introduced me to a couple of cute girls, Gina and Marissa—and to a weird guy named Zach with orange streaks in his hair. Then, as we walked to our lockers, Manuel insisted I have lunch with them at noon. If Manuel only knew how grateful I feel that I won't have to hide in the library again.

Mr. B. has already written the *Math Riddle of the Day* on the white board, but I'm not prepared for what comes next. "I've got it!" the blonde guy in the front row yells out. After he repeats the correct answer, he dashes over to Mr. B.'s desk, picks up the small mallet next to the gong several times. The crashing sound brings a huge smile to Mr. B.'s face while several students stomp their feet and cheer. I can imagine Mr. B. at the family dinner table, hitting a gong every time his children answer one of his riddles about polynomials or some other algebraic term.

We spend the entire period working on the quadratic formula. Mr. B. asks Mark, a geeky-looking guy, to work out a problem on the board, but when he can't figure it out, Mr.

B. asks if anyone knows how to use the formula correctly. Although I know exactly where Mark screwed up, I don't raise my hand. The last thing I want is for everyone to think I'm some kind of show off. Instead, I listen quietly as the smart girl in front of me explains what I already know. Science turns out to be very boring because Mr. Riley lectures the *entire* period about the *Scientific Method*. But when I get to English, the time seems to go by really fast. Mrs. Harrison puts us in pairs so that we can present our claims on the causes of global warming and its effect on the environment. My partner is Tyler, a tall, nerdy student who knows research methods like I know math. I end up hitting it off with him because he's quiet like me, and doesn't mouth off like some of other people in class.

At lunchtime, I hurry to meet Manuel and Zach in front of the gym. While Zach stuffs his mouth with potato chips, Manuel explains that we're eating over by the football field. The sound of hip-hop music grows louder as we approach the bleachers, where two dudes are busy eating their lunch.

"Hey, Chuy," Manuel greets the skinny guy, who is wearing a faded Rolling Stones T-shirt that is at least two sizes too small. "This is Moses. He's new at our school."

The redheaded guy at Chuy's side grins. "*Híjole*, Jesus and Moses together. Wait till I tell my Mom."

"Yeah, Red. It's a holy day for sure," Manuel says sarcastically, and we find a place to sit on the bleachers.

"So where are you from?" Red asks as I stare back at him. I've never seen a Chicano with red hair before.

When I tell Red I'm from Salinas, the freckles on his face light up like fireflies. "I've always wanted to visit the Steinbeck Museum."

"Man, you and that crazy museum stuff," Chuy says, his bulgy eyes almost popping out of their sockets. "I hear there's big-time gangs over there."

Pretending I haven't heard Chuy's remark, I gaze at Red. "I've been to the Steinbeck Museum. Twice. It's got some cool stuff."

"Have you read any of Steinbeck's books? We're reading *Cannery Row* in my English class," Red says.

I'm about to explain that I've read all of Steinbeck's novels, when Manuel interrupts suddenly. "Did anyone notice the tight dress Marissa was wearing this morning?

"She looked *trucha*," Chuy says, smacking his lips together while Red and I exchange a disgusted look.

"Did anyone watch the fight last night?" Zach pipes in. "Man, Herrera kicked ass."

As Zach and Manuel describe every gory detail of the final round, I picture Herrera's fists up in the air like a fearless gladiator. Although I can't stand boxing, I pretend to be interested. By the time lunch is over and we head back to our classes, I begin to feel as if I'm a member of their group.

∽ ∽ ∽

I've just come out of P.E. when I realize I've forgotten my binder for computer science, so I head back to my locker. When I get there, I notice the two girls standing next to me. They seem to be watching every move I make. The short, chubby girl has a cell phone in her hand. She points it at me, whispers something to her friend that I can't make out. I slam my locker door shut and glare at them.

"What's your problem?"

Startled, the chubby girl quickly slips her cell phone in her pocket as they hurry down the hallway. *Chismosas*, I think to myself as I pause at the water fountain. I'm bending down for a drink when I hear a thick voice behind me.

"That's him, dude. It's so cool his dad's in prison."

Waves of anger rush through my body and I spin around to face a big, husky guy wearing a Raiders jersey. He must be a football player. He's showing something on his cell phone to his buddy. I yank the cell phone out of his hand and stare. It's the photo of me with Dad in his blue prison shirt, the same photo from my binder. The caption underneath reads: *It's the new guy with his Prison Dad.*

Cursing loudly, I fling the phone against the wall. The husky guy's cheeks flush. He calls me a dumb-ass as his friend rushes to pick up the broken phone. I lunge at the husky guy, punching him in the face. His friend tries to jump in, but I yell at him to back off. I'm about to take another swing, when Mr. B. suddenly pulls my arm back with one hand.

"Stop it, Moses!" he shouts. More students gather around us. "What's going on here?"

The same chubby girl that I saw earlier points her finger at me. "*He* started the fight. Owen wasn't doing anything."

"Dude's crazy," Owen says as he wipes his bleeding lip with the back of his hand. "He went off on me for no reason at all."

Mr. B. tells Owen to go to the nurse's office. Then he calmly orders everyone back to their classes. Soon we are left alone in the hallway.

"Is that true, Moses? Did you start the fight?"

I lower my eyes, refusing to answer.

"I'll have to take you to the Dean of Students," Mr. B. says, shaking his head sadly.

My knees feel weak as I take a seat in Mr. Marshall's office. What if I get kicked out of school for good? What if we have to move again because of me? Mom will be pissed. She's got a new job and Carmen likes her new school. What if I've screwed it all up? And then there's Dad. Why does everything always have to be about him?

Mr. Marshall's words bring me back to the present. "Now, Moses," he begins in a stern voice. "I want you to tell me exactly what happened."

The words are stuck in my throat. I suddenly wish I were back in Salinas with Arturo, watching a Lakers game or shooting pool at Ralph's Place.

"Nothing happened," I say, fidgeting with the zipper on my backpack.

"You mean you just punched a guy for no reason? You're off to a very bad start, Moses." Mr. Marshall leans onto his desk, adjusting the wire-rimmed glasses on his flat nose. "It's your first week at Roosevelt. Are you sure there isn't something you wish to say about this?"

When I don't say anything, Mr. Marshall slowly rises from his desk. "I have no recourse but to suspend you for three days. I'll have to call your mother."

Later, when Mom walks into the main office to pick me up, she doesn't say a word to me until we're outside.

"Moses, tell me why you did this. It's not like you to start a fight." Then the words pour out of her, "I want to know exactly what happened."

I shrug my shoulders and avoid looking at her. "Some guys were making fun of me, no big deal."

Mom pauses for a second to grip my arm tightly. "Tell me the truth, Moses. That's all I want to hear."

I stare into Mom's soft brown eyes. If I could only tell her about the photograph. But I can't. It would only hurt her. "They were talking trash, you know, cause I'm the new guy."

Mom's eyes fill with tears. "Wait until you father hears about this."

"Oh, yeah?" I say in an angry, bitter tone. "What's he gonna do? Break out of prison so he can come scold me?"

FOUR
Moses

I wake up thinking about the fight. I should've trashed that picture of me and Dad a long time ago. It must've fallen out of my binder, and then one of those idiots uploaded it. This is the first time I've ever been kicked out of school.

Last night I heard Mom crying in her bedroom like she often does, except that this time I didn't know if she was crying because of Dad or me. Sometimes I want to run to her side, beg her to leave Dad and to forget all about him, to live her life and be happy. But I know it would be useless. Once, I heard Mom admit to one of her prison lady friends that she'll do whatever it takes to wait for Dad, that she'll never abandon him. All I know is that I wouldn't be in this mess if it weren't for him.

When I walk into the kitchen, I see the long list of chores waiting for me, written on a piece of paper stuck to the refrigerator: empty the trash, wash the dishes, make the beds, etc. Mom even wants me to vacuum the *entire* apartment. I serve myself a bowl of cereal and take it into the living room. I turn on the Sports Channel. When they show a newsclip of a fight that broke out between two NBA players, I think about that stupid football jerk and his bloody lip. It's probably all over school by now.

∾ ∾ ∾

I'm almost finished vacuuming the hallway when the phone rings. It's Mom calling during her lunch break.

"Did you do everything on the list?"

As I name off everything I've done, I remember the time I took off downtown with Arturo, ignoring her boring list. Mom was livid. She grounded me for an entire week.

I'm brought back to reality when Mom says she left meatloaf for me in the fridge. "Have to go back to work now," she states hurriedly. "Don't forget to remind Carmen to do her homework before she goes out to play."

I've just hung up the phone, when it rings again. It's Mrs. Bates, my counselor.

"How are you, Moses?"

I gaze down at my sneakers, wondering if she really wants to know the truth. I see a small ball of hair on the carpet. If I know Mom, she'll spot it right away.

"I'm fine," I say, bending down to pick it up.

"I wanted to talk about the fight. According to your school records, you've always been a stellar student."

"Yeah, well, things change . . ."

"Moses, can you tell me what provoked the fight?"

"Just *new guy* stuff."

Mrs. Bates takes a long, deep breath before she continues. "I'm going to post your assignments online for your classes so that you won't fall behind."

"Thanks, but I wouldn't bother. We don't have a computer."

My thoughts turn to last summer, when I worked at Burger King and put all my money in a savings account.

Mom's car broke down and I had to withdraw most of the funds to help pay for the repairs. Although Mom didn't want to take my money, what else was she going to do? So there went my dream of having my own laptop.

"Not to worry. I'll call your mother and ask her to come by for your assignments."

After we hang up, I have some of Mom's meatloaf. Then I kick back on the couch with a book I found at the library about Attila the Hun, this cool-looking dude on a horse, waving his sword. He was King of the Huns, a ruthless warrior who subjugated many tribes during the Roman Empire. If only I were a warrior like him, then maybe I wouldn't be locked up in this dumpy apartment.

I'm in the middle of a raging battle between Attila and the Visigoths when Carmen walks through the front door. "I'm hungry," she shouts, letting her backpack slide to the floor. I reluctantly close my book, and she follows me into the kitchen.

"I made a new friend. She lives upstairs," Carmen states as I hand her a peanut butter and jelly sandwich. "Can I go play with her?"

"Mom says you have to do your homework first."

"I don't have any," Carmen says, reaching up with her left hand to wipe away some crumbs from the corners of her mouth.

"You better not be lying," I warn as Carmen quickly stuffs the rest of her sandwich into her mouth so that she can hurry outside to play.

Just as I am about to pick up my book again, there are several light knocks on the door. I take my sweet time, and when I finally open up, I find Manuel standing in the doorway.

"Hey, what's up? Can I come in?"

"Yeah, I guess so," I mumble as Manuel follows me into the living room and takes a seat on the sofa next to me. He pulls out a small envelope from his sweatshirt pocket and hands it to me. "I think this belongs to you."

"What is it?" I ask, opening the envelope. I can feel my face turning red as I stare at the Polaroid. "Tell me who you got this from, so I can beat the crap out of them."

"Chuy found it in the bathroom. Someone had taped it to the wall."

I clench the photograph and toss it on the floor. "When I find out who did this, I'll kick their ass."

"You know, bro, you don't have to lie about your dad."

"How would you know? It's really none of your business."

"Listen, dude. I'm on your side. Besides, one of my uncles is in prison."

I stare into Manuel's eyes, wondering if he's making this up to make me feel better.

"Yeah, my uncle Willie. He was real young . . . got involved in a burglary. He ended up in prison, then they just kept adding more time. I think he's in for life."

We're both quiet for a moment. I can hear the toilet flushing in the apartment above us.

I swallow hard, "My dad's in for life too," I confess.

"That's hard shit. I know 'cause of my *tía*. They move my uncle around a lot."

I wonder if I should tell Manuel the entire story, but he's suddenly on his feet.

"Listen, bro, I've gotta go. I told my dad I'd help him change the oil in his car 'cause my brother Rudy's too lazy.

Now that he's going to college, he says he doesn't have time for anything else except his girlfriend."

After Manuel leaves, I try to read a few more pages, but I can't concentrate. I keep thinking about his uncle Willie and my dad. I was in junior high when Mom finally felt I was old enough to know the truth about Dad. She told me he used to hang out with gangbangers, that he was always in and out of juvenile hall. Then one night, Dad was involved in a robbery where he and his friends held up a 7-Eleven. The cops picked them up, found drugs on them and that's when Dad received his *first* prison sentence. He got out and met Mom not long after. They married, and she got pregnant with me. Everything was fine until Dad started hanging out with his old friends. I must've been around five years old when Dad went back to prison for life. The cops stopped him one night and they found drugs on him again. Dad was sentenced twenty-five years to life in prison. "Three strikes and you're out under California law," Mom said. After that, we went to live with my grandma in East L.A.

By the time Mom gets home, I've pushed Dad completely out of my thoughts, but the moment I see her tired face, the bitterness returns. As she slips off her white shoes and massages the bottom of her feet, Mom asks, "Where's Carmen?"

"She didn't have any homework so I let her go play with her friends." I've always wondered why Mom let herself get pregnant again. I'm glad they took away the conjugal visits at the prison, or otherwise who knows how many more kids would have to endure this miserable life.

"Your counselor called—I picked up your assignments on my way home." Reaching for her purse, Mom takes out an envelope and hands it to me. "Now do you have anything you want to tell me about the fight?"

"Why can't everyone just lay off me!?" I shout, hurrying off to my room and slamming the door behind me.

Later that night, I hear Mom's muffled cries again as I walk to the bathroom. I'm filled with guilt all over again.

FIVE
Ray Gutiérrez

It took me several hours to straighten out Justin Martin's schedule, but I'd managed to get him in the classes he needed next semester. My counseling position at Roosevelt was definitely easier than being director of the Teen Resource Center. I'd felt devastated when funding for the Male Voices Project had been cut and the Teen Resource Center closed. It seemed so unfair that anytime the economy sunk, the first thing they did was cut the programs for the poor and disadvantaged. I'd tried to keep in touch with a few of the students, but when my Aztec drumming class ended, I had to focus on getting another job. Now here I was, at Roosevelt, surrounded by white students who acted as if they'd never seen a Chicano teacher with long hair before.

There was a light tap on my door. "Come in," I said. The door opened and Micaela Guzmán, a small girl with long, black hair appeared. She was one of the first students I'd met during Open House.

"Mr. Gutiérrez, can we talk to you for a minute?"

"Sure thing."

Micaela and two of her friends stepped inside my office. I recognized the tall girl with the smooth, dark brown skin. Zakiya was Tyrone's sister. I'd met her one evening when I'd given him a ride home from the Teen Center. The Latina girl next to her with the braided hair looked vaguely familiar, but I couldn't quite place her.

"Mr. Gutiérrez, we all belong to MEChA," Micaela stated. "I'm the president, and we came to see you because our advisor, Mr. Sousa, moved to another district."

Zakiya chimed in next. "So we were wondering if you'd be our new advisor?"

"Yeah, Mr. Gutiérrez. I'm Karina, the treasurer," the Latina girl finally spoke. "My cousin Edgar used to go to the Teen Center, and he really liked you *a lot*. He used to talk about all the cool stuff you did with them."

I had a sudden flashback to awards night at the Teen Center. Karina had come with Edgar and his family. How could I possibly forget Edgar? *And* his best friend, Kiko! They were both determined to obtain their high school diploma. Edgar was always talking to the other students about staying away from drugs and gangs. That's why I'd selected him as peer leader.

"How is Edgar doing?"

"He's doing so good," she said with a smile. "He graduates this year and says he wants to get a college diploma. He says he owes it all to you."

"Edgar is a smart kid—he did it all by himself." I turned my gaze toward Zakiya. "And I heard Tyrone's at Laguna University."

"Yeah, he really likes it, only now he thinks he's Mr. Big Stuff."

"We've gotta get back to class," Micaela interrupted as the first bell rang. "So what do you say, Mr. Gutiérrez? Will you be our new advisor?"

"I'd be honored. I was a 'Mechista' myself. Let me know when your first meeting is scheduled. I'll be there." All three girls cheered in unison as they hurried out of my office. Smiling to myself, I reached for Juan Díaz's folder while I waited for his mother to arrive for our meeting.

Ten minutes later, Mrs. Díaz was sitting across from me. It was impossible to ignore her swollen eyes underneath the heavy mascara and green eye-shadow.

"I don't have a lot of time. The bank's short on tellers today, so they only gave me a half hour," she said, fidgeting with the leather strap on her purse.

"No problem," I said, holding out Juan's recent progress report. "I called you in because Juan is failing his classes and his teachers are very concerned. I wanted to find out if anything was going on at home."

Mrs. Díaz lowered her eyes for a brief moment, letting out a long, deep breath. "Juan's been having a hard time. I've tried everything, but I can't get him to listen to me anymore." Her voice broke and the tears began to slide down her pale cheeks. Handing Mrs. Díaz a tissue, I waited for her to regain her composure. "My husband left us this summer and we haven't heard from him since then. Juan was real close to his dad."

I thought about the Círculos, rap sessions we held every week at the Teen Center, and the time Jimmy and Kareem had confessed that their dads had walked out on their moms. Although they tried to act tough, as if it didn't bother them, I could see the hurt in their eyes. Then there was Marcos, the sixth-grader who was living in a hotel with his single parent. Too many young men with absent fathers.

I reached out to pat Mrs. Díaz on the hand. "Maybe I can talk to Juan. Before I came to Roosevelt, I worked at a local teen center where many of the boys were struggling with this same issue."

"Juan's always been a good student," Mrs. Díaz said, sniffling. "I know he's feeling bad inside, but every time I try to talk to him, he shuts me out."

"Don't you worry, I'll do everything I can to help him."

As soon as Mrs. Díaz left, my thoughts turned to my son, David. I had tried to reach him on his cell all weekend, but I kept getting his voicemail. I'd finally called Angela, who was her usual cold and uncooperative self. When I mentioned inviting David to spend Christmas break with me, she insisted he was very busy with basketball. It was as if Angela didn't care about my relationship with my son. I knew I'd hurt her with my drinking, but I'd been sober now for almost ten years. Why couldn't Angela forgive me? Why couldn't she understand that I loved David more than anything? Frustrated, I glanced at my watch, realizing it was time for lunch.

I was nearing the teacher's lounge, when I heard someone call out my name. When I turned around, Mrs. Bates greeted me.

"Hello, Ray. Do you have a few minutes?"

Mrs. Bates was one of the most popular counselors at Roosevelt. Students often praised her for standing up for them when no one else would. She was real, authentic. After our first faculty meeting, she had pulled me aside to say that it was about time the administration brought diversity into our staff.

"I wanted to talk with you about the new student, Moses Vargas. He seems like a good kid, but he was suspended for fighting last week."

"So I heard. Do you have any idea what caused the fight?"

"Moses refuses to talk about it, but apparently someone texted a photo of Moses and his dad all over the school."

"What's so wrong about a photo of Moses with his dad?"

"His dad's in prison."

I couldn't help but think back to all the homeboys I'd grown up with whose dads were in prison. We thought it was cool back then. It wasn't until after I'd gone from one juvenile detention center to another that I'd realized it wasn't so cool at all. Then when I saw a twelve-year-old kid get killed in the neighborhood, I knew I didn't want to end up dead or locked up in prison.

"What can I do to help?" I asked.

"I was wondering if you could try talking to him."

"Yes, of course. Do you know where he lives?"

Mrs. Bates nodded, handing me a slip of paper. "Moses lives here in Laguna with his mom. And thanks, Ray—I'm so glad you're on our staff."

SIX
Ray Gutiérrez

I recognized the low-income apartment complex because I'd given Tyrone a ride home several times from the Teen Center. Now the faded brown stucco had been painted a bright green that reminded me of the Mexican limes my mother often used for cooking. There were several new rosebushes and clusters of red, pink and white geraniums that lined the front of each unit. Parking near his building, I climbed the stairs to the second floor. I could hear the faint sound of Mexican *norteñas* coming from one of the apartments. I knocked twice and a young girl who was holding a large, black spoon in her tiny hand opened the gray, wooden door.

"Hi, there," I said, as she tilted her head to the side, her stringy, brown hair jiggling like spaghetti.

"Who are you?"

"I'm Mr. Gutiérrez from Roosevelt High School. Is Moses home?"

"Carmen, who is it?" I heard a voice call out. Seconds later, a petite, dark-haired woman appeared at her daughter's side. Mrs. Vargas was wearing a pair of black jeans and her short hair was pulled back in a red hair band that made her appear too young to have a son in high school.

"He's Moses' teacher," Carmen said. She looked as if she was trying to figure out exactly what I wanted.

As we shook hands, Mrs. Vargas said, "Moses didn't tell me his teacher was visiting,"

"I'm a counselor at Roosevelt. Moses didn't know I was coming,"

"Please come in."

Following her inside the modest apartment, I took a seat on the small black couch. Mrs. Vargas sat across from me on the armchair, nervously rubbing her hands together.

"I'm sorry for not calling first, but I was hoping I could talk to Moses."

"You're our first visitor," Carmen interrupted. "Moses is in his room—I'll get him." As she bolted out of the room toward the hallway, I noticed Carmen was already dressed in a pair of yellow pajama bottoms with happy faces all over them. I had to smile, remembering how David used to prance around the house in his favorite G.I. Joe pajamas.

Mrs. Vargas stared at me, her face lined with tension. "Is this about the fight?"

"Yes, it is. But I'm only here to offer my help."

Carmen suddenly reappeared. "He's coming. Is that a real feather?" she asked, staring at the bone choker around my neck. Mrs. Vargas flashed Carmen one of those dreaded *Mom* looks that I recognized from my own childhood.

"Yes, it's an eagle feather that one of my Navajo friends gave me."

Just then, Moses walked into the living room. He was dressed in a pair of torn jeans and a red Forty-Niners jersey.

Moses was taller than I had imagined, but the only resemblance I could find to his mother were his wide, brown eyes. Moses' words were harsh. "What do *you* want?"

"I was hoping we could talk about what happened at school last week."

"I have nothing to say about it," Moses said, turning around and exiting the room before I could say another word to him.

Mrs. Vargas shook her head sadly while Carmen smiled up at me. "Want to eat with us? My mom makes the best lasagna."

The thought of a home-cooked meal seemed to quiet the rumbling in my stomach. "I don't want to inconvenience anyone, but it sure smells delicious."

"It's no problem at all," Mrs. Vargas smiled. "Please join us. I just need to make the salad."

"Want to see my rock collection?" Carmen asked as she clapped her hands several times.

"I'd love to," I said, watching her dart out of the room only to return moments later, cradling a large shoebox. Sitting cross-legged, she began to line up rocks of different shapes and sizes on the carpet.

"Ever thought of being a geologist one day?"

"Moses always asks me that," Carmen said, holding up a flat, oblong rock with a hole in it. "I found this one at the beach last summer."

While she was explaining how she was going to turn it into a necklace, I heard Mrs. Vargas call out for Moses to set the table.

Five minutes later, we were all seated at the round formica table. I could tell by the menacing look on Moses' face that he was very unhappy about the fact that I was still there.

"You were right, Carmen. This is the best lasagna in the world. And it's nice to not have to eat alone."

"Don't you have a family?" Carmen asked.

"I'm divorced, so I live by myself, but I have a son named David. He lives with his mother."

"Does he come see you?"

"Stop asking so many questions," replied Moses.

"It's all right," I defended her. "David's still in high school, and very busy with homework and sports. But I'm hoping he can come for the holidays."

"I wish I could see my dad every day," Carmen said, her eyes getting watery.

The chair made an abrupt screeching sound on the linoleum floor as Moses stood up. "Why can't you shut up for once?" he scolded his little sister. Then he stormed out of the kitchen, leaving a half-eaten slice of lasagna on his plate.

Mrs. Vargas tried to soothe Carmen's hurt feelings. "Don't listen to your brother. If you're finished eating, you can go watch one of your Star Wars movies."

A smile reappeared on Carmen's face. "Want to watch with me?"

"Maybe later," I told her. "First, I'm going to help your mom clean up, because if I don't move, I'm going to explode."

As I was standing next to Mrs. Vargas at the sink, drying the dishes, she quietly thanked me for trying to help Moses. "He's never gotten into a fight before. I think he misses his dad more than he's willing to admit."

"Does he see him often?"

"No, he can't. Moses, Sr., is in prison. That's why we moved here."

I felt a tightening in my chest as Mrs. Vargas blinked back the tears.

"Moses was only five when his dad got a life sentence. He really doesn't know his dad very well. When he was little he always went with me to visit him, but now that he's older, he refuses to go."

Mrs. Vargas handed me the last dish.

"I was hoping Moses had told you what happened, that someone texted a picture of him with his father. They wrote *Prison Dad* below it. It was circulated throughout the entire school. That's what started the fight."

Mrs. Vargas took a long, deep breath as she leaned against the counter. For a moment, I thought she was going to faint.

"I wish Moses had told me the truth. I know he has been very upset because we had to move from Salinas," Mrs. Vargas whispered. "And he's always trying to keep his dad a secret."

"With your permission, I'd like to start seeing Moses on a regular basis at school. He could really benefit from talking to someone."

"Yes, maybe you can help him," she sighed.

~ ~ ~

Later that night, as I was watching the evening news, I tried David's number.

"Hello."

"How are you, son? Your mom said you're busy with basketball."

"Yeah, I am."

"That's great. I called because I was wondering if you could spend Thanksgiving weekend with me. I've got this new job, new place. We could go out to eat at a nice restaurant."

"Not sure if I can," he said. "Grandma's planning this big dinner, and you know how Mom is—she might get pissed."

Why was it always about Angela? Weren't my feelings just as important as hers? I tried to remain calm. "Will you at least think about it?"

"Sorry, I can't." The line suddenly went dead.

Frustrated, I thought about Moses and his dad, and wondered if my own son would ever learn to forgive me.

SEVEN
Moses

On the first day back at school, I almost lose it when I run into the football jerk and his friends in the hallway. I'm about to cuss them out when they turn around and head in the opposite direction. *Cowards*, I think to myself, wondering if I should go after them, but I don't want to get suspended again. I've already given Mom enough grief.

During science, Mr. Riley is lecturing about the Periodic Table when my name is called on the intercom to report to the main office. I try to ignore the whispers as I walk to the teacher's desk and wait for Mr. Riley to write me a pass. For a few seconds, I think about hiding in the bathroom like I used to do in third grade when the class bully was after me. Only now I can't do that.

∽ ∽ ∽

In the main office, I hand Mrs. Holmes my pass. "Mr. Gutiérrez wants to talk with you," she says, pointing to his office across the hallway. I wonder why Mr. Gutiérrez can't mind his own business. Didn't he get the message the other night, that I don't want anything to do with him? His door is slightly ajar and I catch a glimpse of him standing next to a filing cabinet.

"Hello, Moses. Come on in and sit down."

Taking a seat on the empty chair across from his desk, I rudely ask, "What do you want?"

"Just wanted to see how it's going so far. It was nice meeting your mother and little sister the other night. Dinner was great."

I know Mr. Gutiérrez is trying to make me feel comfortable, but I refuse to respond. Instead, I glance around his office, pausing to study the framed photograph on the wall: Mr. Gutiérrez is standing in the middle of a group of guys, and they're all smiling. One guy even has his tattooed arm draped around Mr. Gutiérrez's neck.

"Those are some of the boys from the Teen Center where I worked last year. We took that picture on our last day together."

"Oh, yeah?" I can't help but notice that some of them look hardcore, as if they belong in prison with Dad.

"The Teen Center closed down and I don't see much of the boys anymore. A few of them are at the Continuation School. And the tallest one, Tyrone, is enrolled at the university." Mr. Gutiérrez's voice suddenly grows soft. "But some of the boys didn't make it."

"What do you mean they didn't make it?"

"Well, a couple of the guys are in juvenile hall and another one went back to banging with his homeboys."

"That'll never happen to me," I say, shuffling my feet. "I'm not gonna be a loser like my dad." Why did I have to go and mention him? Now for sure he'll try some of his shrink talk on me.

Mr. Gutiérrez leans forward, his owl eyes on me. "Would you like to talk about your dad?"

"No, I wouldn't. Can I go back to class now?"

"Wait, there's something I want to ask you. Would you like to come to a MEChA meeting this Friday? It's an organization for students. I'm the new advisor."

Shaking my head, I get up and hurry out of his office before he has time to ask me some more stupid questions. Screw Mr. Gutiérrez and his friendly chat.

∾ ∾ ∾

Later, we're at the bleachers eating lunch when Chuy says, "Heard Mr. G. called you in."

I fight the urge to slap his pimpled face. "Can't people mind their own business?"

"*Chisme* travels fast at Roosevelt," Chuy says, his beady eyes on me.

"Don't listen to him," Red says. "Mr. G. is real cool. He's always talking to us about getting a college degree."

"He told me he's the new advisor for MEChA. He wanted me to go to a meeting."

"*Órale,* you oughta check it out. We're all part of the club," Manuel says. "And plus, there's some hot babes there like Marissa."

Red rolls his eyes as Chuy and Manuel exchange a high five. "That's not what MEChA is about," he says. "MEChA does a lot of good things. Last year, we raised money to buy Christmas gifts for single-parent families. Now with Mr. G. as our advisor, it'll get even better."

"Think about it bro," Manuel interrupts. "Our next meeting is on Friday."

∾ ∾ ∾

P.E. turns out to be boring as hell because it started to rain and we have to play badminton in the gym. By the time I get to my computer science class, I'm ready for a challenge. After she explains the new program, Mrs. Stern orders us to work in pairs to design a new website. I end up with Scott, who's some kind of computer genius. I have to keep telling him to slow down. When Mrs. Stern hears me telling Scott that I don't have a computer at home, she says, "We'll have to do something about that." Slightly embarrassed, I ask Scott a question while Mrs. Stern moves on to another group. If she only knew how long I've been trying to save up for a computer. But, then again, Mrs. Stern is a teacher. What would she know about being poor?

∾ ∾ ∾

After school, I'm watching Jeopardy while I do my math homework. Mom walks through the front door. "*Hijo*," she says, taking off her coat as if it weighed a hundred pounds, "you shouldn't be doing homework with the TV on. Where's Carmen?"

"She went to her friend's house. She left a phone number on the table next to the mail."

Just as I thought, Mom goes straight to the kitchen and returns seconds later, waving a letter in her hand. You'd think she'd just won the lottery from the smile on her face.

"I got approved! We can go see your dad this weekend."

"I'm not going. You can take Carmen."

"You have to come, *hijo*. It's your dad's birthday."

"Oh, yeah? And where has *he* been for all my birthdays?"

There are tears in Mom's eyes as I gather up my books and escape to my room. I drop my books on the floor next to the door and turn the radio up as loud as it will go.

Why do I have to hurt Mom like that? Why can't I accept things the way they are? Sometimes I hate Dad so much that I wish I never had to hear his voice or see his face again.

EIGHT
Moses

On Friday, Manuel and Red talk me into going to the MEChA meeting with them at noon. I just couldn't bear the thought of eating alone and wasting my time thinking about Dad's birthday tomorrow, not that I give a damn about it. But last night when I walked past Mom's bedroom, it sounded like she was crying again. It seems like now she cries every single night. After that, I couldn't go back to sleep. I lay awake for the longest time wondering if I should just suck it up and go with Mom and Carmen to the prison.

I've never been inside the multi-purpose room where the MEChA meeting is being held. It's a large room adjacent to where the school buses park. I really like the wall lined with windows and the nice view of one of the huge mountains that surround Laguna. I've never been into science or geology like Carmen, but I thought it was really cool to learn that these mountains were once volcanoes.

There are about half a dozen students gathered, munching on potato chips and eating their sandwiches. Mr. Gutiérrez or Mr. G., as the students call him, is leaning against the edge of the desk talking with Marissa.

"Hey, *chula,*" Manuel greets Marissa, who glares at him, but she gives me a big smile that makes me slightly

41

uncomfortable. Arturo would always scold me for not paying attention when a girl had the hots for me. Guess he wanted me to be a ladies' man like him.

"Glad you could make it," Mr. G. says as Red compliments him on the bright *guayabera* he's wearing. It reminds me of a photograph Mom once showed me of Grandpa Vargas. He was wearing one just like it, except it was beige.

After we're seated, a short girl with thick, black hair moves to the front of the group, signaling for the meeting to begin. "Thanks for coming. I think everyone knows me. I'm Micaela, the president of MEChA. We're *so* happy Mr. Gutiérrez agreed to be our new advisor."

Chuy and Manuel let out a few annoying whistles as she continues. "I'd like to introduce this year's officers. Well, the ones that are here today." Micaela then points to the tall, African-American girl seated to her right. "Zakiya is the Vice President."

Zakiya flashes everyone a smile, revealing a set of perfect white teeth that remind me of the Colgate commercials.

Next, Micaela introduces the thick girl seated next to Chuy. "Karina is the treasurer."

Blushing, Karina lowers her eyes. Micaela turns the meeting over to Mr. G., who moves back toward the front of the group.

"I'm thrilled to be your new advisor. I once belonged to MEChA—at the university, of course. They didn't have MEChA in high schools back then."

"Man, you must be old," Chuy says, his voice sounding like fingernails scraping a blackboard.

Manuel pokes Chuy on the side with his elbow. "I bet he's not too old to kick your butt."

A girl behind him giggles as Mr. G. continues speaking.

"As most of you know, this is my first year at Roosevelt, but I've been working with young people since I graduated from the university. My last position was at the Teen Center here in Laguna. Unfortunately, it closed down, but I'm hoping to provide the same leadership and guidance on our campus. And even if I'm not your counselor, you can come see me any time."

Micaela promptly takes over the meeting again. "Thank you, Mr. G. The first thing on our agenda is this year's fundraising. Any ideas?"

Zakiya is the first one to offer a suggestion. "We could have a car wash."

"All the other clubs do that already," Karina says in a soft quiet voice.

"Yeah," Chuy agrees with her. "Besides, I get tired of washing my *jefito*'s car all the time." Red calls him a lazy bum and it takes all my will power to refrain from calling Chuy something worse.

"What about a burrito sale?" Marissa asks. "We could do it around Cinco de Mayo."

I'm startled when Marissa turns to look at me with her bright, emerald eyes. "What do you think, Moses?"

Manuel gives me a light kick under the desk and I can feel the room suddenly heat up.

Aware that all eyes are on me, I say, "Sure, why not?" Chuy suddenly leans forward ready with a comeback, but I give him a menacing look and he backs off.

When Mr. G. brings up community service, everyone turns their attention back to him. Julie, the tall, Anglo girl sitting behind Zakiya, waves her hand in the air.

"I have a great idea. My aunt visits my cousin at the local prison every month. She said that sometimes people don't wear the right clothes and the officers don't let them in. But there's a place next to the prison called *Friendly Helpers* where they can borrow clothes to change into. My aunt said they're always running out of clothes. What if we were to do some kind of project to help the organization *Friendly Helpers* gather more clothes?"

"What a great idea," Micaela tells her. "Can you get some more information?"

I can feel huge knots forming in my stomach as if I need to throw up. There's no way in hell I'll join MEChA. It's bad enough the whole school knows my dad's in prison. They can collect their own stupid clothes.

The moment the bell rings, I rush out the door before any of the guys can catch up to me. In the bathroom, I splash water on my face, wishing I could disappear off the face of the earth.

∾ ∾ ∾

When I get home that afternoon, I find Mom seated at the kitchen table with Carmen. They're sorting change before it goes into a small, plastic purse that she's allowed to take into the prison. Mom glances up at me from the piles of quarters, dimes and nickels around her.

"Hi, *m'ijo*. I got off early today so I could go by the bank."

"Want to help?" Carmen asks as I reach for a soda from the refrigerator.

I shake my head, trying not to show my disgust. When I was Carmen's age, I used to think it was fun helping Mom count all that change too. Now the sight of all those coins remind me of prison vending machines and prison dads.

I feel Mom watching me as I take a long drink from my soda.

"You are going with us in the morning, right? *Ándale, hijo. Es su cumpleaños.*"

Why is it that Mom always uses Spanish when she's trying to convince me to do what she wants?

"You have to come, Moses," Carmen pleads with me. "It's Daddy's birthday."

Carmen's sweet little voice tugs at my heart. Unwilling to shatter her illusion of happy, birthday celebrations, I reluctantly tell her, "I'll think about it." The next thing I know, Carmen leaps to my side, hugging me and telling me I'm the best brother in the world.

∽ ∽ ∽

On Saturday morning, I slowly climb out of bed and put on my nerdy, black slacks and my long-sleeved brown shirt. I always wear the same clothes to the prison. One time I felt so embarrassed when I had to change clothes. It was at Soledad State Prison. An officer insisted my shirt was the same blue as the inmates. I ended up having to wear the ugliest plaid shirt I've ever seen, and it was one size too small.

Mom and Carmen are waiting for me when I walk out of my room.

"*Hijo*, you'll have to eat on the way over. I'm number twenty today—we need to hurry."

On weekends, all the prison moms line their cars up alongside the freeway as early as 6:00 a.m., waiting for the gates to open so they can be the first ones to get a number. Then they go back home to pick up the kids.

Lucky me, I think to myself as Carmen hands me an egg burrito and we rush out the door after Mom.

NINE
Moses

As we turn into the parking lot, there are groups of women hurrying out of their cars to line up in front of the Gatehouse. Some of them are carrying babies and diaper bags while others tug at the hands of sleepy-eyed children. I can't help but notice the contrast as we get off the car: behind us there are majestic mountains with hilltops, and a freeway that leads to the ocean, but directly in front of us there is a huge sign that says *California State Prison* with a high, chain-link fence that surrounds the entire facility.

Mom quickly finds our place in line behind two Latina women who are speaking both English and Spanish. The lady with the curvy body and ruby red lipstick pauses to introduce herself.

"I'm Cristina and this is my friend, Lupe. First time here?"

"Yes," Mom says as I stare at Cristina, who is wearing so much make-up on her face that she reminds me of a clown.

Reaching up to untangle a strand of hair that is caught in one of her gold hoop earrings, Lupe says, "This is one of the best prisons in California. It's not like Chowchilla or

Folsom. You get to sit at any table you want. And the officers are nicer here, *más gente.*"

"They even have a big patio in front that has picnic tables," Cristina offers. "It's real nice. They open it up at eleven. Me and Frankie like to sit there because you can see the mountains."

Then, as if they were tour guides, they begin to describe all the different prisons they've visited. I wish I could tell them to shut up.

"Have you filled out your visitor's pass?" Cristina asks Mom. "They're over there on the small stand by the door."

"No, I haven't," she replies.

As Mom hurries to fill out her pass, Lupe reaches out to pat Carmen on the head. "My little Joey is about your age, but I couldn't bring him today. He has a bad cough."

"I'm ten," Carmen proudly admits as I turn around to gaze at the line, which almost extends to the parking lot. If only I were home sick like Joey, or back in Salinas with Arturo . . .

Mom makes it back in line just as the officer comes out to open the doors. We slowly file into the Gatehouse so the officers behind the counter can process us. When we arrive at the front of the line, Mom eagerly hands the middle-aged officer her driver's license, along with our birth certificates. It takes several minutes to input all of our information on the computer since it's our first time at this prison.

When the officer finally stamps our pass, we move across the room to another line so that two different officers can inspect our belongings. I'm all too familiar with the routine; take off shoes, jackets, belts, remove all jewelry—guess they want to make sure we're not carrying any weapons or explosives. Only then are we allowed to move to the final line where we wait to pass through the metal detector.

Mom lets out a huge sigh of relief when the three of us go through without any problems. But as we're putting our belongings back on, the metal detector suddenly goes off. I'm embarrassed for the young woman, whose face turns crimson when the officer warns her that she'll have to change if she's wearing an underwire bra.

After the officer stamps our wrists, we pass through the solid, prison door. I gaze up at the barbed-wire fence ahead of me that leads to the guard tower as I stand with the other women and children. I wonder which is worse, being all alone in that tower or being locked up in a prison cell?

Once we're inside the main building, we hand our Visitor passes to the officer behind the counter. Then we finally pass through another prison door and into the visiting area. We hurry after Mom to one of the cheap, white plastic tables near the back.

"*Hijo*," she says, when we sit down. "Carmen and I are going to buy some drinks. Wait here so that no one takes our table."

While I wait for them, I survey the visiting room. It seems more spacious, but maybe it's because the tables are smaller and more evenly spread out. In Salinas, the tables were so close together that you could hear everyone's conversation. But what surprises me the most is the large colorful mural on the front wall. It has a small pier next to an oceanfront and it's lined with fishing boats. All I ever remember seeing in other prison visiting rooms were plain, dull walls.

Just as Mom and Carmen return from the vending machines, Dad comes out through the back door where all the inmates have been waiting for their names to be called. Dad's face breaks into a huge smile when he sees us.

"There's Daddy!" Carmen squeals, as she and Mom rush over to meet him.

I watch Dad hand his prison ID to the officer behind the window before he turns to lift Carmen high up in the air. When he pulls Mom into his arms, I'm suddenly filled with pity for all the prison wives. They're only allowed to hold their wives at the beginning and the end of each visit.

"*Hijo,* I'm glad you came," Dad says, patting me on the back before he takes the empty chair between Mom and Carmen.

I force a smile out, taking in his neatly shaved face, the half-moon scar above his left eyebrow. One time Mom showed me a picture of Dad when he was my age. It was as if I were staring at myself in the mirror, the same dark, wavy hair and thick lips. Arturo always liked to tease me, saying I had big "sugar lips" that all the girls wanted to kiss.

"Happy birthday, Daddy," Carmen says, leaning closer to Dad, who places his arm around her and squeezes her little shoulder. Then Dad turns to look at Mom, stroking her hand tenderly.

"How's the new job?"

"I like it a lot," Mom says. "I have a good work schedule and my supervisor is very nice."

Why is it that Mom is always trying to protect Dad? Maybe she can fool him, but not me. I know for a fact that even if she hated her job, she wouldn't tell Dad the truth.

"Daddy, I have a new friend," Carmen interrupts. "Her name's Tammy and she lives next door." Then Carmen describes how they both collect rocks and like to read the same kinds of books.

"And what about you, *hijo?*" Dad asks, eyeing me closely. "How do you like your new school?"

I want to tell him the truth, but one glance at Mom, makes me hold back. "It's fine," I mutter, tapping my fingers nervously on the table.

Before Dad can ask another idiotic question, Mom grabs her plastic purse, insisting that it's time to get some food before the vending machines are empty. As they leave, a voice on the intercom announces that the outdoor patios are open. It makes me sick to my stomach watching all those boys and girls cling to their prison dads as they head outside. I remember when I was their age, how I used to daydream that one day I'd come home after school and Dad would be there waiting to help me with my science project. Poor little kids. If they only knew what lies ahead for them. But then again, maybe it's better that they don't.

"We brought you this," Carmen says, handing me a burger. Mom always shares a sandwich with Carmen, and it bothers me. She pretends she's not very hungry, but I know it's her way of making sure the quarters last for the entire weekend.

While we eat, Dad talks about his "cellie," or cellmate who everyone calls Johnny Boy. "He's a lifer like me, from San Bernardino. A dropout from the Mexican Mafia. Johnny Boy has been in prison for almost thirty-five years. *Es buena gente.* He's the one who helped me get the job in the paint department."

"*Qué bueno*," Mom says, relief on her face. Mom worries like crazy every time Dad gets moved to a new prison. But I guess you can't blame her, it's not as if he's vacationing at a four-star hotel.

When Carmen begins to complain about all the math homework she has every night, Dad says, "Have Moses help you—he's the brains in the family."

He waits for me to acknowledge his compliment, only I don't say a word. How would he even know what I'm good at? It's not like he's ever visited any of my schools or met my teachers.

As soon as we've finished eating, we go outside to the small patio in the back. All of the benches are taken, so we end up having to fall in line with all the other couples, who are strolling around in circles. We're coming around the small tree at the far end of the patio, when I spot a tall, African American girl that I've seen at Roosevelt. We've never talked and I don't even know her name, but there she is, sitting on a bench next to an inmate and a woman who has to be her mother. Our eyes meet for a brief moment and I feel an instant connection between us. We circle around the patio for the second time and I look for her again. A different couple is seated there now.

Carmen starts to whine that she needs the bathroom, so we go back inside. While I sit and wait at the table, I glance around for the girl from Roosevelt, but she's nowhere in sight.

"Look, Moses, it's Dad's birthday cake," Carmen's voice brings me back to the present. She and Mom are each holding a small, vending machine carrot cake. At Carmen's insistence, we sing "Happy Birthday" to Dad. Then he hands each of us a slice of cake on a plain, white napkin.

We're almost finished with our pathetic birthday celebration when two of Dad's prison friends stop at our table to congratulate him. Dad introduces the tall, red-haired guy with the long ponytail as Prowler. Then he introduces the short Chicano with the tattooed neck as Güero.

Shaking my hand, Güero says, "Your dad's always bragging about how smart you are, that you're going to college."

Prowler pats me on the back. "Yes sir, wish I'd listened to my old man, not dropped out of school."

The minute they leave, Dad shakes his head sadly. "There's some guys in here who can barely read and write." Dad's face suddenly brightens as he stares into my eyes. "*Hijo,* I'm almost finished with my G.E.D. And I'd like to take some correspondence courses after that."

"*Qué bueno,*" Mom says, squeezing Dad's hand. Carmen claps her little hands, but all I can feel is irritation. Why is Dad wasting his time? He's never going to get out of here anyway.

After that, Mom and Dad go for a short walk on the front patio while Carmen and I play several rounds of checkers. At 3:30, they announce that it's time for visitors to leave, so we all make our way to the front, squeezing in among all the inmates who are frantically saying goodbye to their families. Dad hugs Carmen first, giving her a kiss on the cheek. Then he embraces me.

"Thanks for coming, *hijo,*" he whispers in my ear.

When an officer suddenly shouts the final call for us to leave, Dad pulls Mom into his arms and hastily kisses her.

Then he falls in line with the other inmates, waving back at us as they file out of the visiting room.

"Mommy, can we come tomorrow?" Carmen sniffles as Mom wipes away a tear sliding down her face.

"Yes, *m'ija,*" Mom nods.

I stare at her wishing the earth could swallow me up.

TEN
Moses

The sound of Mexican *cumbias* coming from the apartment next door wakes me up the next morning. I think about Arturo and how he always used to listen to *corridos* and *rancheras*. One time when I asked him why he liked Mexican music so much, he explained that he grew up with it. His grandpa would always listen to Antonio Aguilar and Vicente Fernández in their home. I still couldn't understand why he preferred old people's music to hip-hop or jazz.

After I take a nice, long shower, I go into the kitchen to eat breakfast. Although it's nice to have the apartment all to myself, it seems deathly quiet without Carmen's constant chatter. Sometimes, though, she gets on my nerves with her endless questions. She's probably talking Dad's ear off now. I'm so damn glad I didn't have to waste my entire weekend at that disgusting prison.

All of a sudden, I hear the lock turning on the front door and moments later, Carmen walks into the kitchen followed by Mom. "Can I have some cereal?" Carmen asks as Mom drapes her red wool coat over the kitchen chair.

"What happened?" I ask, handing Carmen a bowl. Then I wonder why I even bothered to ask; I've seen that look on Mom's face a thousand times before.

"They're on lockdown," Mom says. "We got up to the visiting room and waited for almost two hours until they finally told us that visitation was cancelled. *Ay, m'ijo*, there were these two ladies who drove all the way from Anaheim. I felt so bad for them."

I'm about to make a smart-ass remark, when Carmen interrupts.

"I made a new friend—her name's Crystal."

"Her mother's name is Rosie. She's a real nice lady," Mom says. "They just moved here too, so we exchanged phone numbers."

Great, I think to myself, *another wasted life, another stupid lady waiting for her loser husband.*

"I even bought two photo ducats so we could take pictures with him." She reaches up to wipe a tear from the corner of her eye.

"Don't cry, Mommy," Carmen says softly.

Like a movie flashing before me, I remember the countless lockdowns and weekends with no visits, Mom waiting and waiting for the phone to ring. One time, the lockdown lasted almost two weeks. It even made the evening news; some kind of prison riot. I thought Mom was going to lose it then. I could hear her footsteps late at night pacing around the apartment. It wasn't until Dad was finally able to make a phone call that Mom acted normal again.

I can't take this any longer. I push out my chair and say, "I'll be back later." I hurry through the living room and walk out the front door before anyone can stop me.

After several minutes of breathing in the clean air and the sweet smell of lilacs, the pounding in the back of my head starts to subside. I gaze at the perfect stucco homes with their manicured yards and two-car garages. Why can't I have a normal life with a normal family? Why do I have to go through the same miserable crap year after year? Why can't Mom think about Carmen and me for once? Why does everything always have to be about him?

I soon find myself downtown, where the busy streets are filled with the sound of city buses and honking. This is definitely not like Salinas. Here the streets are lined with expensive stores, restaurants and trendy outdoor cafes. It's obvious that Laguna caters to tourists and rich white people who spend their money on stupid stuff. At least in my old barrio you could find Mexican stores where they sold *pan dulce* and homemade tamales. Not here, that's for sure.

Nearing the end of Main Street, I spot a Lakers banner on display, so I go over to the small NBA store. When the sales clerk, a Lucha Libre look-alike, asks if I need any help, I politely explain that I'm just looking. Taking a moment to admire the large purple and gold Lakers flag hanging on the wall, I head to the back of the store. "*Híjole*," I whisper as I stare at the price tag on the new Black Mamba jersey, sounding like my mom. If only we weren't so damn poor, then I could buy every single Kobe jersey in the store.

Frustrated, I go back outside, turning the corner onto a quieter side street. I'm passing a Middle Eastern clothing boutique, when I come to Cameron's Used Book Store. I pause to admire the display of John Steinbeck's books on a cart outside, I pull out my wallet from my jeans pocket. Ten bucks. "*Good,*" I whisper to myself.

As soon as I step inside, I'm surrounded by shelves of books. There are even *piles* of used books on the floor. Feeling like a little kid at a Fourth of July carnival, I stroll up and down the aisles scanning one title after another. I'm instantly drawn to a section with books about different countries. I spend the next hour leafing through books on Spain, China, the Middle East until I finally settle on a paperback about the Caribbean Islands.

I'm standing at the counter. The bearded hippie guy is handing me my change when I feel a light tap on my shoulder. I turn around to find the pretty girl I saw yesterday at the prison.

"Looks like we keep running into each other," she says, handing her money to the cashier.

I suddenly wish Arturo were with me. He was always such a smooth talker with the girls. "Yeah, maybe," I hastily answer, hurrying toward the exit before I make a fool out of myself. Only the mystery girl is very persistent, and she follows me outside.

"Hey, wait up. I'm Dalana. I've seen you at school. You're the new student, right?"

By now, my thoughts are scrambled up in my head like puzzle pieces. I'm sure she heard all about the fight. "Yeah, so what?" I tell her, walking faster.

"I didn't mean it like that," Dalana blurts out, catching up with me. "Where are you headed?"

"Back to my apartment."

"Me too. I live near City Park. It's just a few blocks from here. Want to walk me there?"

Feeling tongue-tied, I nod. Besides, I'm in no hurry to get back to the apartment.

"Well, do you have a name?"

I can't help but grin. "Moses, like in the Bible."

While we wait for the traffic light to turn green, Dalana asks, "Was that your dad yesterday?"

"If you can call him that," I answer bitterly.

"That was my dad, too. How long has your dad been in prison?"

"Ever since I can remember."

"Me too," Dalana sighs. I recognize the sadness in her voice and, for a second, I want to put my arms around her like Mom does when Carmen wakes up from a bad dream.

We're both quiet as we cross and continue walking. I glance at a fearless skater gliding down the street. What I wouldn't give to be like him, not a single care in the world except for my skateboard.

"My mom was so upset today because we couldn't get in to see my dad," Dalana says, jarring me back to reality.

"Yeah, I know. My mom totally freaks out when they're on lockdown. Sometimes I want to slap her out of it."

Dalana suddenly pauses in her steps. "Don't say that, Moses. Lockdowns are scary; terrible things can happen."

"Sorry," I apologize, wishing I could take back my stupid comment. Why can't I keep my big mouth shut?

We approach an intersection at the corner of City Park and Dalana points to the olive green apartments.

"I live over there. You can turn back now."

"Cool," I say, wishing I could stay with her a while longer. But then again, maybe she thinks I'm a total jerk.

Dalana gently places her hand on my arm. "Thanks, Moses. And if you ever need to talk, let me know." She darts across the street, waving back at me.

ELEVEN
Ray Gutiérrez

I was in the middle of scheduling several college campus visits for the junior class when my thoughts drifted to my conversation with Mrs. Díaz. I remembered the promise I'd made to her, so I sent out a request to meet with Juan Díaz.

Fifteen minutes later, a handsome young man with black, curly hair appeared at my door. "Come on in, Juan," I said, pointing to the empty chair. "We haven't met, but your mom and I spoke last week."

Juan sat down, shuffling his feet several times. "Yeah, she told me."

"It appears you're failing several classes. However, your school records show that you've always been a very good student, so I wanted to talk with you about this."

Juan jerked his head up, his dark eyes smoldering with anger "What's it to you? You don't even know me."

"You're right, I don't know you. But I do care." I heard him mutter a cuss word, but I wouldn't let it get to me. If Juan only knew how often the students at the Teen Center had tried to get me to back down. "Your mom mentioned you've been having a rough time since your dad left."

Juan shot up out of his seat. "Why'd she have to open her big mouth? My dad has nothing to do with this—I'm late for P.E."

And before I could stop him, Juan was gone, slamming the door behind him.

Reaching up to massage the back of my neck, I glanced at the photograph on the wall. I'd been hired to work at Roosevelt because of my experience with marginalized youth, only now I felt stuck. How was I going to get through to Moses and Juan? A sudden thought entered my mind. I reached for the phone and dialed.

As soon as I heard "Hello," I jokingly asked, "How's the old *vato* doing?"

"Is that you, Ray?" I heard Mike chuckle in the background.

I'd first met Mike years back when I attended the first meeting of Los Compadres in Santa Barbara. It was there that I first learned about the concept of the Círculos.

"To what do I owe this *milagro*?" he asks. "How are you? Long time no see."

"I'm doing great, been meaning to drive down to Santa Barbara to attend a meeting, but I've had a lot going on— new job, moved to another city. How's the *familia*?"

"Everyone's great. Junior is finishing up at City College and Maggie's a freshman at UCSB. Janice and I are alone most of the time now. How's David?"

Although Mike knew all about the divorce, over the past few years, I'd avoided mentioning how strained my relationship with David had become. I'd felt embarrassed. How could I be so successful with other teens, but not with my own son?

"It's David's senior year—he's busy with basketball and trying to keep up with his classes. But listen, I'm calling because I need your expert advice again. I'm working as a Counselor now at Roosevelt High School in Laguna and I've got some *raza* students that I can't seem to reach. So I was thinking of starting the Círculos here. What do you think?"

"That seems like a very good idea. If I remember correctly, you used them at the Teen Center, right?"

"Yes, and they were a huge success, only I'm not sure if the school administration here will go for it."

"Why wouldn't they?

"Well, because it's a predominantly Anglo school. And you know how public schools are about non-traditional programs."

"Listen, Ray, if you only knew about all the opposition I had to face when I founded Los Compadres—from city council members to educators. They all thought I was crazy. What's the principal like? Is he or she a good guy?"

"Yes, he is," I agreed, thinking back to my first interview with Mr. Marshall. He'd asked the kind of questions that led me to believe he was honest and fair, that he sincerely cared about the well-being of his teachers and students.

"Well, there's your answer. Go talk to him about it."

As soon as we hung up, I took Mike's advice and headed straight for the principal's office. Mr. Marshall was seated at his desk working on his laptop.

"Mr. Marshall, do you have a few minutes?"

"Absolutely, Ray," he said, gazing up at me. "Come on in. How are things going? All I've heard are praises from the staff."

As I took a seat across from him, I realized my hands felt sweaty. "Thank you, everyone's been very helpful and supportive."

"I'm glad to hear that. I have a meeting in five minutes," he said, glancing at his watch. "Now, tell me, what's on your mind? "

"I have a couple of Latino students who have some serious things going on in their lives. One of them, Moses Vargas, is the new student who was recently suspended for fighting. The other one is Juan Díaz. He's close to flunking out."

Mr. Marshall raised his eyebrows. "I remember the fight. And if my memory serves me right, Juan Díaz is a sophomore."

"Yes," I nodded. "And so, I have this idea—I belong to a non-profit organization called Los Compadres Network and they use support groups called Círculos or Circles, to help empower troubled youth. I used the Círculos with my students at the Teen Center and they were very effective. I was wondering if I could start one here at Roosevelt."

Closing his laptop, Mr. Marshall was on his feet. "Sorry, Ray, time for my meeting. I'll need more information before I can give you a yes or no. Is there a website you can direct me to where I can read about this organization?"

"Yes, I can send you some links that describe the National Compadres Network and the different programs they provide for at-risk males."

"Good, send me that information as soon as you can and I'll get back to you."

∾ ∾ ∾

At noon, I went to the MEChA meeting feeling hopeful and inspired by Mr. Marshall's words. While many of the same students had returned, I was disappointed that Moses wasn't among them.

After Micaela went over the minutes from the last meeting, she directed her next question to Julie.

"Do you have any more information about your idea of collecting clothes for *Friendly Helpers?*"

Julie's face was beaming. "Yes, I talked to my aunt and she thought it was a really good idea. She gave me their number."

"Nice work," Micaela complimented her.

"Since I'm your club advisor," I said, raising my voice slightly and moving closer to the students, "I'd be more than happy to contact *Friendly Helpers.*"

"*Órale,* Mr. G.," Manuel quickly agreed.

Thanking me, Micaela added, "Why don't we talk to our parents about this and start gathering up some clothes?"

Marissa waved her hand in the air. "My mom always saves the clothes that my little brothers outgrow. I'll talk to her today."

"Hey, baby, you can text me anytime, you know?" Chuy said, blowing her a kiss.

"Shut up, you little weasel," Marissa shouted back as the room filled with laughter.

After the meeting, I was making my way back to the main quad when I spotted Moses coming out of the library.

Although he tried to pretend that he hadn't seen me, I hurried after him, forcing him to pause.

"We missed you at the MEChA meeting."

"I've got better things to do," Moses said, avoiding my eyes. Then, before I could say another word, Moses was gone, leaving me frustrated as hell.

TWELVE
Moses

I've never understood how anyone could hate math. I've always loved working with numbers, and Mr. B. is so cool; he knows I love it as much as he does. My math teacher at Salinas High was so boring that everyone messed around when he was writing on the board.

I'm thinking of all this, walking out of English class, when I meet up with Dalana and Zakiya.

"Hey, Moses," Dalana says, motioning for Zakiya to go on ahead without her. "Would you like to have lunch with me?"

"Sure," I answer, wondering how anyone in the world could say no to her.

"Why don't we meet over by the quad next to the gym?"

"That's cool, but I need to drop off my books at my locker first."

"Me too," Dalana says, giving me a huge smile before she disappears down the hallway.

Manuel and Chuy are waiting for me at my locker. "Dude, make it fast. I'm starved," Manuel says as he stuffs a handful of Doritos in his mouth.

"Sorry, I'm not eating with you today."

As I shove my books into my locker, Chuy glances up from his cell phone. "What's up? You got a hot date today?"

"None of your business," I tell Chuy, who raises his bony fist in the air as if he wants to duke it out with me.

"No problem, bro," Manuel grins. "I'll see you after school."

On my way over to meet Dalana, I stop off at the snack cart. There are so many different drinks to choose from that I'm not sure if I should buy Dalana a juice or a soda. I finally settle on two lime Gatorades, but as I stretch out my arm to pay, I wonder if I put on enough deodorant this morning. What if my body odor repels Dalana? If only I had some of that good-smelling cologne Arturo would spray on himself every time he hit on a girl.

When I get to the quad Dalana is already on a bench waiting for me. There are only two other students on another bench nearby, but they're busy making out. The minute she sees me, Dalana waves, so I hurry to join her. I catch a whiff of her sweet smelling perfume as I hand her a Gatorade.

"Thanks," Dalana says. "I love lime. How are things going?"

"Way better." Dalana's long dark hair is braided today. I try not to stare but she looks even prettier in the sunlight.

"How's your mom?" Dalana asks, nibbling on her sandwich. "My dad was finally able to get a call out last night, so mom's not as panicky."

"Dad still hasn't called. My mom's all freaked out." I almost can't believe I'm talking openly about my dad with someone else. When I lived in Salinas, Arturo was the only one I could trust.

"I'm sorry," Dalana whispers. "I'm sure they'll be off lockdown soon."

"What do I care anyway? It's nothing to me."

Dalana lifts her chin up, her eyes boring into me. "Moses, you don't mean that, do you?"

I gaze down at my scuffed up sneakers. If there's one person I would never want to hurt, it would be Dalana.

Placing her hand gently on my arm, Dalana says, "In my World Cultures class, Mrs. Coates showed this documentary about the Middle East. It's called *Promises*. It's about this journalist who interviewed all these young kids about how they felt about the Israeli/Palestinian conflict. Some of their fathers were in prison camps. It made me think of our dads."

"How is that?" I ask, the harshness gone from my words.

"It showed what these families had to endure to get to the prison camps. This one Palestinian family had to pass through all these Israeli checkpoints where they were searched like crazy. Then they travelled for hours to the camps and when they finally got there, they were only allowed to see their dads for thirty minutes." She stopped and stared into my eyes. "So you see, Moses, we haven't got it so bad. At least we can spend an entire day visiting our dads. You should check out the movie. It's probably online or at the library."

"Yeah, maybe I will."

We're both quiet for a few moments, then Dalana says, "Zakiya said you're thinking about joining MEChA."

I'm quick to react. "I just crashed a meeting, that's all."

"Moses, you ought to think seriously about joining it or some other club. It really helps. I'm on the Robotics team. We do a lot of cool stuff like programming robots. We even go to competitions." Dalana goes on to describe the last competition they went to in Berkeley and how they tied for first place.

When the bell rings, we carefully gather up our trash. As we head back toward the main quad, I wonder if maybe I should give MEChA another chance.

In computer science, the substitute teacher gives us permission to work on our websites. But instead of doing that, I Google the documentary Dalana mentioned. I'm surprised to find so many film reviews and video clips about *Promises*. The synopsis on the website even calls it the "best documentary ever done" because it's told from the perspectives of seven Palestinian and Israeli children. By the time I check out several more film reviews, I'm convinced that I should take Dalana's advice.

After school, I'm on the bus going home when Chuy, who is sitting behind me, says, "So you like upper-class chicks now?"

Turning around, I grab him by the collar of his sweatshirt. "Shut up, you little punk," I sneer.

Chuy's eyes are bulging out of their sockets and I can smell his bad breath.

Manuel pulls my arm back. "Chill out, dude. You know this school's nothing but *chismelandia*."

Before I let go of Chuy, I tell his pimpled face, "Dalana and me are only friends."

"All right, all right," he mumbles, wiping the sweat off his upper lip as Manuel calls him a weasel.

∾ ∾ ∾

While we're having dinner that evening, the phone rings. Mom hurries to answer it and the second I hear her say "Yes," I know it's a collect call from the prison.

"It's Daddy," Carmen exclaims, pushing her chair back. But I order her to stay put and finish her spaghetti.

After a few minutes, Mom comes back into the kitchen looking completely transformed. Her eyes seem brighter and there is a glow on her face as if she's just won a million bucks in the lottery.

"That was Chente, one of your dad's friends. He called to say your dad's fine, and that his quad should be out of lockdown by next weekend."

Carmen waves her fork in the air. "Yay, we can go see Daddy and I can tell him about the 100 I got on my spelling test!"

"Yes, *m'ijita*," Mom says, patting Carmen on the head as she sits back down to eat. "He'll be so proud of you."

I'm about to say something sarcastic but then the image of kids in the Middle East forms in my mind. I think of the hell they have to go through just to visit their dads at the prison camps. Maybe Dalana's right. Maybe we haven't got it so bad.

THIRTEEN
Moses

Third period is almost over when my name is called on the intercom to report to the main office.

"What did you do now?" Mark, who is sitting behind me, whispers into my ear. His thick garlic breath is repulsive. It's no wonder the girls in class look away when he talks to them.

When I arrive at the main office, I find Mr. Gutiérrez standing at the counter talking with Mrs. Holmes.

"You're just the guy I wanted to see," he says in a serious tone.

For a second, I wonder if I should panic, but I haven't been in any trouble at all since the fight. Besides, I promised Mom I wouldn't break any more rules.

Once we're seated in his office, Mr. G. says, "How's your mom?"

"Is that why you pulled me out of class? So you could ask about my mom?" I give him a hard, cold stare. Why doesn't he leave me alone? There are hundreds of other students he can bother at Roosevelt. Who does Mr. G. think he is anyway, some kind of savior like Jesus?

Mr. G. leans forward in his chair, an amused look on his face. "Actually, I wanted to tell you about a new after school group I'm starting up. I was hoping you'd participate."

"I can't, I have to take the bus home right after school," I say, thinking he'll get off my back. Except that Mr. G. is a hardass.

"That's not a problem. I can give you a ride home."

Feeling cornered, my gaze falls on the small red figure dangling from the center of Mr. G.'s beaded necklace. "Is that some kind of bear?"

"Yes, it's made of red jasper. A friend gave it to me when I was going through a rough time. The bear symbolizes strength and power."

I find myself suddenly wishing things could be different. If only I had some of those special bear powers. Glancing up at Mr. G, I ask, "So what kind of group are you starting?"

"It's called a Círculo."

"A circle? That sounds stupid."

Mr. G. smiles. As he begins to describe the Círculos, his eyes widen. He emphasizes how much his students at the Teen Center liked them. After a few minutes, he fixes his eyes on me again. "So what do you think, Moses? Will you come to our first meeting?"

"Why me? There are a bunch of other students at Roosevelt."

"Because I believe you have a lot to offer and the Círculos can help you."

I'm quiet for a moment and watch a single ray of sunlight shine directly on the red bear. Maybe the Círculos will help me find my own power and strength.

"Okay," I finally agree, hoping I won't regret it. "I guess I could check it out."

During lunch Manuel can't stop talking about the Círculo either. When Chuy opens his sleazy mouth to say he thinks it's a lame idea, Red doesn't waste a second in coming to Mr. G.'s defense.

"Mr. G.'s just trying to help us. Besides, he knows what he's doing. He's not a *pendejo* like you."

Chuy tries throwing his banana peel at Red, but he catches it and flings it back. We all laugh as it hits Chuy and he cries, "You could've poked my eye out!"

By the time I get to computer science, I've forgotten all about Mr. G. and his "Circles." Mrs. Stern explains that today we're going to learn about blogs so that we can add one to our websites. Some of the guys in class make weird noises as she shows us a variety of sports blogs. When Mrs. Stern shows a fashion blog, Janell, who is the class drama queen, loses it completely. Her scream is so loud that I have an instant flashback to a scene from *Exorcist 3*.

After that, Mrs. Stern gives us time to work alone. I'm looking at a travel blog, imagining that I'm on top of Teotihuacán when Mrs. Stern pauses at my side.

"Moses, I heard you mention that you don't have a computer at home. Would you be interested in a refurbished computer?"

"What's that?" I ask, turning to face her.

"It's a computer that was no longer working, but we had it repaired. Every year, Roosevelt donates a few of these refurbished computers to students who are interested in technology. So what do you say? I can have one ready for you tomorrow after school."

I can feel my heart beating like a runaway train. I've been wanting a computer for so long that I almost can't believe it. "That would be awesome," I answer and Mrs. Sterns hurries across the room to help a student who is frantically waving at her.

∿ ∿ ∿

The moment I step inside the apartment I'm greeted by the sweet smell of oven-baked cookies. It's Mom's day off and Carmen likes to follow her around like a shadow. Sometimes Carmen will even pretend she's not feeling well so that she can stay home from school to spend time with Mom. I go straight to the kitchen, and grab a cookie off the lopsided pile on the table.

"Your favorite—chocolate chip," Carmen says, placing another weird shaped cookie on the baking sheet. Mom is standing next to her. They're both wearing the goofy matching aprons with baby chicks that grandma made for them last Christmas.

"How was school?" Mom asks, glancing up from the cookie sheet.

"Good. Can we get an internet connection?"

"*Hijo,* you know we don't have a computer."

"Mrs. Stern is giving me one of the school's refurbished computers. She's letting me bring one home tomorrow."

Mom's eyebrows shoot up. "*Qué es eso de* 'refurbished'?"

Before I can finish explaining, Carmen rudely interrupts. "Can I use it too? We have iPads in our classroom."

I give Carmen one of my mean brother looks before I turn back to Mom. If anyone knows how long I've been saving up for a computer, it's her.

"Please, Mommy?" Carmen begs. "I can show you how to use the computer!"

"Okay, *hijo*, we can call tomorrow," Mom says to me winking at Carmen.

"Thanks, Mom," I answer, suddenly realizing she *is* on my side and maybe I shouldn't be so damn hard on her. After all, it's not Mom's fault we're in this mess.

FOURTEEN
Moses

Early Saturday morning, Mom comes into my room and yanks the covers off my head. "Moses, *hijo,* Carmen woke up with a fever. She'll have to stay home while I go visit your dad. I gave her some Tylenol. If she starts coughing, give her some cough syrup. It's on the table."

I force my eyes open, but before I can reply, Mom is gone. It never fails. Dad always seems to ruin everything in my life. But I guess, I'd rather watch Carmen all day instead of hanging out at the prison. The door swings open again and Carmen plops down on the edge of the bed. Her hair is all messed up and she smells like she bathed in Vicks VapoRub, Mom's remedy for everything.

"Can I watch cartoons?" Carmen asks.

"Go ahead," I answer, pulling the blankets back over my head.

I'm dreaming I'm on a curvy mountain road in a small red car and I'm about to drive off the edge, when Carmen's voice rescues me. "Moses, can I have some hot chocolate? My throat hurts." Then Carmen releases several pitiful coughs that make me think she's only faking it.

"Chill," I say, realizing it's almost eleven. "I'm getting up right now."

Once I've showered and dressed, I grab a bologna sandwich and join Carmen in the living room. She's watching Nickelodeon. When she begs me to play a game with her, I agree as long as she turns off the TV. For the next hour, we play Monopoly. I've just finished buying the video arcade when the phone rings. It's grandma calling from East L.A. "*¿Cómo estás, hijo?* I know your mom's not there, but I wanted you to let her know that tomorrow I'll be going to see your dad. My *compadre*'s son was transferred to the same prison and they invited me to go with them. Tell her I won't be spending the night because I have a doctor's appointment on Monday."

"Okay, Grandma. I'll tell her." I can feel my body stiffen, knowing exactly what Grandma is going to say next.

"*Hijo*, I'll see you there tomorrow, *¿qué no?*"

The words shoot out of my mouth. "I can't, have a lot of homework."

Grandma's voice is barely a whisper now and I can hear some sobs in the background. "*Ándale, m'ijito*, please come," she pleads with me. "You know how happy your dad gets when we're all together."

I close my eyes, trying not to think about all the tears Grandma has cried for Dad.

"Don't cry, Grandma. I'll be there," I hear myself whisper. I hand the phone to Carmen and realize I've just screwed myself. There's no way in the world I can break a promise to Grandma.

∾ ∾ ∾

On Sunday morning, Grandma is waiting for us at the Gate House with her *compadres*. She's wearing a loose, flowery dress that makes her look as if she's shrunk an inch since the last time we saw her. After she gives Carmen and me a giant hug, Grandma introduces Mom to Mr. and Mrs. Torres. Then she insists we get in line with them until the visiting doors open.

At exactly nine o'clock, an officer steps out to open the doors. As we go inside to get processed, Mom reminds Carmen for the umpteenth time to not cough until we've gone through the metal detector. The line moves swiftly this morning since there are only a handful of new people to process. Half an hour later, we're inside the visiting area. Today we don't have to race to get a table because Grandma is with us and we're allowed to sit at one of the handicapped tables that are also reserved for old people.

As Mom and Carmen leave for the vending machines, Grandma tells me, "*Hijo, gracias por venir*—your dad will be so happy you came." Then she begins talking about Mrs. Torres and how they both watch the same *novela*. "*Se puso como loca* when I told her that Arsenio had killed the *padrecito*."

While Grandma describes the murder in detail, I gaze around the room. I can't help but think that most families head for church on Sundays, but not us. Here we are in this musty-smelling room that is filled with mostly Black and Chicano families. When Dad finally appears in the visiting room, I can tell by the surprised look on his face that he had no idea grandma was going to be here. As they all rush to meet him, I glance toward the back of the room. Just then, I spot Dalana and her mother standing in front of the coffee machine. I instantly wish I'd worn something else instead of this dull brown shirt.

I'm forced to turn my thoughts away from Dalana and her mom when Dad appears at my side. "I'm so glad the whole family's here," he says, patting me on the back and taking a seat next to Mom. When Dad asks Grandma about the barrio, she begins to complain about how much everything has changed.

"All these gringos are moving in—they even made Don Tiburcio close down his *panadería* so they could put up some new apartments."

"*Sí, Amá*," Dad agrees. "I read about the gentrification that's happening there."

I almost jump out of my seat. I've never heard Dad use words like that before. Mom said he didn't even graduate from high school.

"*Hijo,* I went to the library yesterday," Dad says. "I'm reading this book about the Aztec *códices*."

"Oh, yeah?" I say. Who would've thought Dad liked to read or that they even *had* a library in this god-forsaken place.

After that, the morning seems to go by fast as we listen to Grandma tell stories about her childhood. I never knew my great-grandparents were one of the first Mexican families to settle in East L.A., or as Grandma says, *El Pueblo de Nuestra Señora Reina de Los Ángeles.*

"My *apá* used to have a garden in the backyard with chiles and tomatoes," Grandma explains. "We even had a pig."

Carmen's eyes widen. "What was his name?"

"Porfirio. He was named after *aquel malvado dictador*, Porfirio Díaz," Grandma winks at her.

When Dad bursts into laughter, I see the wide gap on the side of his mouth where he's missing several more teeth. Mom's always stressing about the poor medical care he gets in the prison.

We're eating our vending machine sandwiches when a tall Chicano with a long, dark ponytail stops by our table. He talks with Dad for a few minutes, but his voice is so low that I can't make out what he's saying. After he leaves, Dad says, "Chucho is Apache. He was inviting me to the sweat lodge. He goes every Sunday."

"There's a sweat lodge here?" I ask, trying hard to keep my voice steady.

Dad nods. "We also have a small chapel. There's a lot of *indios* and *indio* wannabes here who go to the sweat lodge."

Mr. G. suddenly appears in my thoughts. "One of the counselors at school is Native American."

Dad raises his eyebrows. "Do you know what nation he's from?"

"I'm not sure, but he wears all this beaded stuff with feathers."

When Dad turns to Carmen and begins to describe Chucho's colorful collection of Macaw feathers, I notice that Grandma purses her lips. I know for a fact that Grandma thinks anyone who doesn't go to church is a heathen.

At three o'clock, the guard announces on the intercom that it's time to put all the games away. As we move toward the front with all the other inmates and their families to say goodbye, I feel a tinge of sadness. Maybe I didn't have such a terrible visit with Dad today.

Back at the Gate House, we get in line for the final time so that the officer can check Mom's driver's license and the stamps on our wrists. We then go outside to wait with Grandma for Mr. and Mrs. Torres. As I turn my head sideways, I spot Dalana exiting the building. Dalana's arm is draped tightly around her mother and they're both crying.

FIFTEEN
Ray Gutiérrez

I was sitting at my desk, going over the letter I'd written to the parents about the Círculos when my thoughts drifted to Tuesday's faculty meeting. It was when Mr. Marshall asked me to describe the Círculos that I felt the bad vibes or *las malas vibras* as my mother would often say. Jeff Nelson, who taught business courses, was the first to speak. "We don't need programs like that at Roosevelt. Our students are different."

"We don't have gangs at our school," Connie Hopper, a teacher I had recently talked with because one of her students was ditching her class, emphatically agreed. "Besides, we have few minority students."

There were several loud gasps in the room as Mr. Bates pointed his index finger at her. "Careful now," he warned. "You're stereotyping Latino students."

By now, the Spanish teacher, Mr. Villamil, was glaring at Jeff and Connie. "Have you forgotten about last year's suicide attempt by one of Roosevelt's star students? And you still think our students don't have any problems?"

"This is not about race—all students have problems," Mrs. Bates added, sounding loud and firm.

Jeff was about to fire back with another remark when Mr. Marshall tapped his pen loudly on the desk.

"As you all know, our student body at Roosevelt is becoming more diverse. This is why we hired Ray in the first place. I want everyone to know that he has the administration's full support for implementing any new programs that will help our students succeed."

My thoughts were instantly pulled away from the faculty meeting when I heard a light tap on the door. Moments later, Susan Harrison stepped into my office. "Hello, Ray. Do you have a minute?" Susan was one of the most popular teachers at Roosevelt. Students were always praising her use of hip-hop music in her poetry and literature classes.

"Sure thing," I smiled back at her.

"I wanted you to know that Jeff's remarks at the faculty meeting were totally out of line. We absolutely need teachers like you at Roosevelt."

"Thanks, Susan. I sure wish everyone else felt that way."

"They'll come around, just wait and see. They're simply afraid of anything that has to do with change, and some of them are still stuck in the McCarthy era."

"I hope you're right," I nodded. In all my years of teaching, I'd learned that standing up to conservative teachers and institutions was not a piece of cake, so it was good to have allies.

"Listen, Ray. I have a student I'd like to recommend for your Circles. Charlie Wiles, he's a sophomore. The only thing is that he's not Latino, he's white."

"That's not a problem," I said. "The Círculos were originally created for Chicanos and Latinos, but they've always been open for all students, regardless of their ethnicity."

"That's exactly what I was hoping you'd say. Charlie has had some problems with drugs, and his parents can't seem to reach him. I already spoke to his counselor, Ginny Thompkins, about your program. She thinks it would be a great idea for Charlie to attend."

"I'm glad you checked with her first. I wouldn't want to step on anyone's toes."

"Yes," Susan agreed, glancing at her watch "Time to go home now, but I'll let Ginny know you approve. She'll talk with Charlie's parents."

Immediately after Susan left, Jan strolled into my office, waving the consent form in the air.

"Mr. Marshall said it's a go," she exclaimed.

"Perfect timing," I said, thanking her. "Do you think you can Xerox the letter and consent form and place them in all the faculty mailboxes by tomorrow morning?"

"Will do," Jan said, raising her hand to salute me as if I were her military commander.

By the time I finally left campus, I was so excited about the first Círculo that I drove straight to Moses' apartment complex. This time it was Moses who answered the door. He was wearing a pair of baggy sweat pants and a faded Kobe Bryant T-shirt. "What do you want?" he asked in a menacing tone.

"Is your mother home?"

"What for?"

It was clear Moses didn't want me anywhere near his family.

Just then, Mrs. Vargas appeared in the doorway. "Mr. Gutiérrez, what a nice surprise. Please come in, you're just in time for dinner."

Muttering a few words that I couldn't make out, Moses was gone before I could say another word to him. As I stepped inside the small living room, the smell of homemade tortillas brought images of my Mexican grandmother standing in front of the *comal*, creating her own small pyramids.

The minute she saw me, Carmen hopped off the couch and ran to my side. "Mom's making *chile con carne*. Will you please eat with us?"

"Sorry, I can't tonight. But maybe next time." Then I turned to look at Mrs. Vargas. "I came by to drop this form off for you and Moses."

I noticed the warmth fading from her eyes as I handed her the envelope. I could imagine the scary thoughts running through her mind.

"There's nothing to worry about," I quickly reassured her. "It's about the Círculos—a support group I'm starting after school. I'm hoping you'll give Moses permission to attend. I've included a brochure describing what they're about."

"Will they help Moses?" she asked, the light returning to her face.

"Yes, I'm certain the Círculos will help him. Mrs. Vargas, please talk with Moses about this, okay? And if he agrees to attend, you'll need to sign and return the consent form."

"Thank you, Mr. Gutiérrez. I'll make sure I talk with him tonight."

Driving back to my apartment, I thought about all the single mothers I'd met at the Teen Center. They had such a huge responsibility to take on: the roles of both mother and father all by themselves. So many young boys without dads. Tomorrow I would call Mrs. Díaz to make sure Juan had given her the consent form. And maybe it wouldn't hurt to call Manuel's parents either. After all, I could use everyone's support.

SIXTEEN
Ray Gutiérrez

On Friday morning, coming out of a meeting, I heard someone holler out my name. I turned around as Manuel ran up to my side. He had a green gym bag draped over his shoulder.

"Hey, Mr. G. Here's my consent form. I'll be at the Círculo after school. And Moses is coming too." Before I could thank him, Manuel raced off toward the gymnasium.

At exactly 2:45 pm , I headed over to the multi-purpose room. After I arranged six chairs in a semicircle, I reviewed my notes. I knew I needed to choose my words carefully in order to gain the confidence and trust of each student.

The first one to arrive was Juan Díaz. He was wearing a pair of khaki pants that reminded me of the ones I wore when I was his age, only mine were two sizes larger. My eyes were drawn to the black rosary hanging from his neck.

"My mom said I had to come or else."

"You won't regret it," I told him, pointing to the chairs in the semicircle. I heard the door open again as Manuel and Moses entered the room.

"Hey, Mr. G.," Manuel said. "Chuy flaked on me, but at least I got Moses here."

"Glad you both could make it."

"It's not like I had a choice," Moses replied, tossing the consent form on the table.

"You both know Juan Díaz, right?"

Manuel grinned. "Yes, we went to the same junior high."

While Manuel and Juan were reminiscing about the time someone lit a firecracker in their Spanish class, a tall lanky student with dirty blond hair walked into the room. This had to be Charlie, the student Susan had recommended. He was carrying a long skateboard with stickers pasted all over it. He pulled out a crumpled consent form from his pocket and placed it with the others.

"Dude, what are you doing here?" Manuel asked with a puzzled look plastered on his face.

"My parents threatened me—that's why," Charlie replied, setting his skateboard on the floor next to his chair.

"I didn't know there were gonna be white kids here," Juan Díaz said with annoyance in his voice.

"The Círculos are open to everyone." I shook my head disapprovingly. "I'm glad Charlie joined us today."

"I still don't understand why he had to come," Juan insisted.

Charlie glared back at him. "Just 'cause I'm white doesn't mean my family is perfect. My parents are poor— we live in a trailer park. My mom works at a laundromat and my dad's a drunk."

"It's time to get started," I said, moving to the center of the group to sit down. "But first, I'd like to say something about my policy of confidentiality. It's very simple—whatever we say in this room, stays in this room."

"Does that mean I can't tell any of my girlfriends?" Manuel said, lightening the mood in the room as Juan called him a *"mil amores."*

Once they were quiet again, I continued. "We always begin the Círculos by stating positive affirmations about ourselves or by stating something we'd like to achieve."

"That's stupid," Juan said. "Why would we want to do that?"

Manuel was quick to react. "Stop cryin' and let Mr. G. talk." I was glad Manuel was on my side.

"Affirmations will help you be a better man. They can help you to become a stronger person, to be grateful for who you are and what you have."

"That's a joke. I don't want to do this crap," Charlie said, pushing his long hair behind his left ear.

"It's not an option, Charlie. You each have to do it, but I'll go ahead and begin with an affirmation I have for myself." Breathing in slowly, I said, "I am proud of who I am."

There were a few snickers from the group, but I ignored them. "I'll give you a few minutes now to think about your own affirmations."

As soon as I let them know their time was up, Manuel eagerly raised his hand. "This is easy, Mr. G. I'm slick with the chicks."

I couldn't help but smile at Manuel's cockiness. "I'll let that one slide for today."

Next, Manuel turned to look at Moses, who was sitting to his left. "Your turn, dude."

"I don't have anything to say," Moses said as he crossed his arms.

"Dude, you've gotta be kidding—you're like a math genius."

Moses tilted his head sideways, deep in thought. "I guess I am good at math. Mr. B. is always calling on me in Algebra."

"I hate math," Juan said, shifting uncomfortably in his chair. "But one thing I can think of is that I babysit my little sister a lot. We play games and stuff. Sometimes she bugs the hell out of me, but I guess you could say I'm a good brother."

Charlie suddenly began to spin the wheels on his skateboard. "I like to play the guitar and write songs," he muttered.

"Dude, that's cool," Manuel said. "Wish I could do that."

I breathed in a sigh of relief. "Thank you for your affirmations. Now I want each of you to share something personal about yourself. I'll go first again." I could feel their eyes on me. "The Círculos saved my life. I was having a hard time—my life was a mess. I was drinking all the time. In the Círculos, I was challenged to confront my feelings and to become aware of who I was and what I needed to do. It was because of them that I was able to join Alcoholics Anonymous, and become the person that I am today."

"That's deep, Mr. G.," Manuel sighed. "I'll go next. Everyone knows I'm the handsomest dude at Roosevelt, that I drive the girls crazy."

"Talk about an egomaniac," Charlie complained while Juan and Manuel exchanged a smile.

His voice barely a whisper, Moses said, "I hate Roosevelt. I hate being a new student and I *really* miss Salinas High."

"Aren't you the guy whose Dad's in prison?" Charlie blurted out.

Manuel was quick to defend his new friend. "What's it to you?"

"Sorry, dude," Charlie said with regret in his voice. "I didn't mean anything bad. I just wish my own dad was locked up. He's a loser—all he does is get drunk and bad-mouth my mom."

Juan leaned forward in his chair. "At least you have a dad, mine took off and left us."

For once, Manuel's words were serious. "I don't know what I'd do if my dad were gone. Sometimes we get into it, but he's always there when I need him."

The room grew silent except for the loud caws coming from the crow perched on the tree outside the window. I knew that I needed to help them find their own voice as I had done with the boys at the Teen Center. "Growing up without a father can be rough. I know because I also grew up without a dad."

Juan's head jerked up. "You did?"

"Yes, my father walked out on my mother when I was born. But I came out all right, didn't I?"

Manuel's timing couldn't have been more perfect. "Have to admit it, Mr. G. You are a little weird."

"I'll second that," Charlie agreed and they all smiled in unison.

It was suddenly clear to me that for the first time today, all four boys had made an important connection with each other, and that made me feel glad. I hoped they felt it too.

SEVENTEEN
Moses

I can't get the Círculo out of my head all weekend. It really pissed me off when Charlie mentioned my dad was in prison, but I couldn't help but feel sorry for him and Juan when they talked about their own dads. Guess I've always imagined that everyone else had the perfect dad, a father they could talk to and who could teach them how to be a real man. It might sound weird, but I actually feel better knowing that Charlie's dad is all screwed up and that Juan's took off. Maybe I don't have the worst dad in the world.

After school on Monday, I'm on the bus when Manuel brings up the Círculos. "It was awesome. Mr. G. might be a little out there, but he's cool with all his Indian stuff."

Zach, who is sitting across from us, tilts his head up and raises his hands in the air saying, "Oh, great warrior, please help me get a girl."

"Bro, that's so insulting," Manuel says, his words sharp as a razor blade. "Haven't you heard of the great chiefs like Crazy Horse or Sitting Bull?"

"You mean the guy on the nickel?" Zach's voice is dead serious.

I shake my head in disgust. Zach is like a lot of people who still believe Columbus discovered America and that the pilgrims were the first "Americans." There's no way I'm going to educate him about Native American history.

Back at the apartment with Carmen, I make sure she's doing her homework before I go into my bedroom and turn on my computer. It's still hard to believe that I have my very own laptop and Wi-Fi that I can use anytime I want. Out of curiosity, I Google "prison blogs." I can't believe it when my search brings up numerous hits. Scrolling down, I scan their titles. The list seems infinite.

What surprises me most is that the prison websites are not only from the United States, but from other countries. Some of these websites even include original poetry or artwork by the inmates. I think back to the drawing of Iron Man that one of Dad's prison buddies made for me on my fifth birthday. I remember hanging it on my bedroom wall and fantasizing he'd help me rescue Dad from prison and bring him back home. It was around seventh grade that I finally threw Iron Man in the wastebasket.

For the next hour, I examine one blog after another. The first is by a man named Tim, who is doing time at a state prison in Kansas for vehicular homicide. Tim recounts his entire story about being drunk and causing the fatal accident that killed an elderly man. Admitting that he is an alcoholic, Tim then gives advice to other addicts like himself, hoping they'll avoid the same tragic mistake. In the final sentences, he apologizes to his wife and two children: *Mary, I am so sorry for hurting you, Mikey and Jenni this way. Please believe me, I'll live the rest of my life making it up to the three of you.* Closing my eyes for a moment, I imagine Dad sitting at a computer and confessing all his sins to the world.

The next website is entirely about Chicanos and African American inmates who are way younger than Dad. Most of them are serving life sentences and, for some reason, all their stories sound the same. One dude, Chente, discusses growing up in South Central: *I always felt as if I were a second-class citizen. I'm very ashamed for what I did, turning to gangs, terrorizing my own community, but it was the only viable path I could see. Gangbangers became my role models.*

I think back to that year in my Social Studies class at Salinas High when we had a discussion about racism and the Jim Crow laws. Some of the students couldn't believe it, but I did. My grandma used to tell me about the "No Mexicans Allowed" signs in restaurants when she was growing up and how bad it made her feel.

One blog, in particular, makes me think about Dad. It is about Ricardo, a lifer, who was released from prison after thirty-five years. In his blog, he describes the terrible guilt he lives with every day for murdering a friend. But what impacts me the most is when Ricardo mentions he is currently completing his Bachelor's degree: *I want to go to law school so that I can help poor people like me who never had money for an attorney.* I remember laughing when Dad wrote me a letter one time from Tehachapi saying he wanted to get a college degree. I thought he was crazy, but now I realize Dad *could* get out of prison one day and change his life like Ricardo has done.

When Carmen opens the door without knocking, I'm about to yell at her, but Mom suddenly appears at her side.

"*M'ijo*, how was school today?" She bends down to massage the back of her right leg. Mom's feet are always aching. Sometimes, they swell up so badly that she has to soak them in ice water for hours. That's when I get real pissed at Dad—if he were around Mom wouldn't have to work this hard.

"Moses was ignoring me," Carmen whines. "He's always on his computer."

"Is that so?" Mom says, winking at me and placing her arm around Carmen.

"I was researching different websites. We're learning about blogs in my computer science class and we're supposed to come up with an idea for our own blog."

"A *blog*?" Mom asks with confusion in her voice.

"I've decided to write about what it's like to have a Dad in prison."

"That's wonderful, *hijo*," Mom says as the phone suddenly begins to ring. "Hurry, *hijita*," she orders Carmen. "It might be your daddy."

A few seconds later, Carmen yells out from the living room, "It's Mrs. Ramírez. Do you want to buy some *tamales*?"

I can tell Mom is upset that it's not Dad calling and I begin to hate him all over again for making her live this way.

EIGHTEEN
Moses

On Wednesday at noon, I meet up with Dalana at the same spot as before, near the auto shop. Today she's wearing a clingy red sweater with a short ruffled skirt. I resist the urge to tell Dalana she looks amazing, like one of those beautiful models on magazine covers. Reality check for me—she *is* a sophomore and I wouldn't want her to think I'm a little punk trying to hit on her. As I sit next to her on the bench, I breathe in the smell of jasmine. How could anyone smell this good?

Finishing the last bite of her sandwich, Dalana focuses her gorgeous brown eyes on me. "Aren't you having anything else besides a soda?"

"I'm not all that hungry," I answer. The truth is that I'm very nervous when I'm around her. What if I get a piece of food stuck in between my front teeth or what if I suddenly start to choke? I'm not willing to take that chance.

When Dalana pushes a long strand of curly hair away from her mouth, I find myself wondering if her lips are as sweet as her perfume.

"Have you seen *Promises* yet?" she asks, gazing up at me.

"No, not yet."

"Well, I think the entire school should see it, especially students like us, with dads in prison."

I instantly glance around to see if any of the students on the benches nearby have heard Dalana's confession. If Dalana only knew how embarrassed I felt at the Círculo last week when Charlie mouthed off about my dad.

"Is it that easy for you to talk about your dad being in prison?" I ask, feeling uneasy.

"Why shouldn't it be easy?" Dalana's voice is tender and soft. "I love my dad more than anything. Besides, all the students at Roosevelt know my dad's in prison. I'm not ashamed of it. He's been in prison for thirty-two years. He did some bad things when he was young, but he's changed. My dad's a good man. Everyone makes mistakes, and I forgave him a long time ago."

Those were the exact same words Arturo would repeat each time I cussed out my dad. Then he would talk about his uncle Ben and how he came out of prison a changed man and turned his life around. If only I could believe that about my own dad.

"Moses, you shouldn't feel ashamed of your dad," Dalana insists. "You should feel proud of him."

"Maybe you're right. Guess that might be why I'm creating a blog in computer science for students whose dads are in prison."

"Moses, that's a terrific idea. You'll help so many kids with it." Dalana's smile fills up the sky like a giant rainbow. "They'll have a place where they can share their feelings about prison life instead of keeping it all inside."

"The only thing is, if I create this blog the entire world will know my dad's in prison."

When Dalana places her hand gently over mine, I feel a warm sensation run through my body.

"Remember what I just said, Moses. You and I have nothing to be ashamed of. Our dads just made terrible mistakes, but they're paying for them now. Are you going to see your dad this weekend?"

"I'm not sure. I really can't stand being there. The guards treat us as if we're crap. It's an ugly place and I really hate going there."

"Your dad needs you, Moses. Besides, there's beauty everywhere. Even in a place like that."

When the fifth period bell rings, I find myself blurting out, "Do you want to go see a movie sometime?" I can feel my left eye start to twitch, but Dalana's smile eases my anxiety.

"Sure, that would be fun."

I have a hard time concentrating on anything during my next class. We're playing basketball, but I still can't believe Dalana actually said yes to me. All I can think about is what kind of movie she might like. The new *Mission Impossible* is out, but what if she doesn't like action movies? Or maybe she'd like to see a comedy instead.

By the time I get to computer science, I'm forced to stop thinking about Dalana when Mrs. Stern interrupts my continuous daydreaming.

"Moses, give me a brief summary of your blog and your objectives for creating it."

First, I tell her about the different prison websites and blogs I've researched online. Then, in a calm, steady voice, I explain, "I'm creating a blog for students whose fathers are in prison. I want to give them a place where they can express themselves."

"I like your idea, Moses. I think your blog will help a lot of young people. Nice work, and do let me know if you have any questions."

"Thank you, Mrs. Stern," I tell her, feeling proud of myself.

As Mrs. Stern moves on to the other side of the room, Marsha, who shares the table with me says "I wish there were more students at Roosevelt like you, not so self-centered all the time."

"Thanks. What's your blog about?"

"It's about one of the local homeless shelters. I'm hoping it will help bring more attention to all the homeless people in our area."

"That's cool," I agree, realizing that I've completely misjudged Marsha. Maybe not all the students at Roosevelt are spoiled white kids.

∾ ∾ ∾

That evening, I'm watching a program about aliens on the History Channel when the phone rings. Irritated, I repeat "yes" into the receiver. I holler out for Carmen to call Mom, who is next door checking on Mr. Aragón. You'd think Mom was a real nurse the way the neighbors are always asking her for help.

After about thirty seconds, Dad's voice greets me on the other line. "Moses, I'm glad you answered. How are you?"

"I'm good," I lie. Now I've missed the end of the program I was watching. Why is it that Dad always calls at the wrong time? But I suppose it's not like he can call whenever he wants.

"Is your mom home?"

"She's next door, but Carmen went to get her."

"Okay, great. *Hijo?*"

"Yes?"

"It's almost Thanksgiving. Your mom and Carmen are coming to spend the day with me. Will you please come with them?"

Just as I am about to repeat one of my usual excuses, I remember what Dalana said to me earlier. Everyone makes mistakes.

"Okay, I'll be there," I whisper, waving the receiver at Mom who is already rushing through the door.

NINETEEN
Ray Gutiérrez

For today's Círculo, we were in the conference room across the hall from the music room. I could hear the faint sound of a piano as I sat down at the center table. Charlie was sitting alone at the table to my left, his skateboard on the chair next to him. His long hair was pulled back in a ponytail and I could make out the tiny, silver cross in his left ear. Manuel and Moses were sharing the same table directly across from me while Juan sat to their right.

"Welcome back. It may feel a little awkward since we can't form a circle, but let's begin with our affirmations. Why don't we focus on what we each want to accomplish. Any volunteers?"

When Juan muttered a complaint, Manuel flicked his chin up at him. "Dude, stop acting like a baby. Mr. G., why don't you go first like the last time?"

"All right, but next time, one of you will have to go first." Pausing for a moment to clear my voice, I began, "I want to support all of my students and make a difference in their lives." Then I fixed my gaze on Manuel, letting him know that he was next.

"No problem," Manuel grinned. "I want to be smart and get a college degree like my brother, Rudy." Turning to look at Moses, he asked, "How about you, bro?"

"Yeah," Moses nodded. "I think I'd like to be a teacher like Mr. B."

Charlie suddenly began to tap his long bony fingers on the table. "All I know is I don't want to be like my old man."

"You're not the only one," Juan agreed, stretching out his long legs under the table.

When I reminded them that we were stating positive affirmations, Juan shrugged his shoulders. "I wrote a poem in English and the teacher liked it. So maybe, I'd like to be a writer one day."

"Then you can write all the love poems for my girl-friends," Manuel remarked with a sly smile.

Juan chuckled as Charlie lifted his head to say, "I'd like to become a world champion skateboarder."

"That's great," I complimented Charlie. The energy in the room had suddenly shifted. "And now I'd like to talk about *La Palabra*. It was one of the first concepts I learned when I attended my first Círculo."

"What does that mean?" Charlie asked in a sarcastic tone. "I don't speak Spanish."

"La Palabra means being a man of your word. It's about being *un hombre noble*, or a noble man who feels good about himself internally and externally, a man who honors and respects women."

"That's deep, Mr. G.," Manuel said, reaching for the comb in his shirt pocket.

Juan looked at me with harshness in his eyes. "But how am I supposed to feel good about myself when my dad's a loser?" he asked.

"Mine's a loser too," Charlie growled.

Moses leaned forward and looked as if he wanted to stuff the words back into Charlie's mouth. "How do you know they're losers? Maybe they just made some bad decisions."

"Look who's talking," Juan said. "Your dad's locked up in prison."

"Yeah, but that doesn't make him a loser."

"Moses is right," Manuel insisted. "My brother has a friend named Tyrone, and *his* dad's an alcoholic. He took off for a while, but he got some help and came back. He's cool now, even goes to AA."

"Yeah, well, miracles do happen," Charlie said sarcastically.

Manuel fiercely defended himself. "People can change. Anyway, bro, you don't know anything. You don't even know what it's like to be black or brown. Tyrone says he's constantly harrassed by cops just because he's black."

"Dude, you're over exaggerating," Charlie insisted as Juan shook his head in disbelief.

Glaring at Charlie, Moses asked, "Haven't you heard of Trayvon Martin, or are you that ignorant?"

Tapping my pen loudly on the table, I ordered everyone to calm down. "We'll talk about racism another time. Let's go back to La Palabra. In Native American culture, women are held in sacred honor. They are revered as the matriarchs, the most powerful members of the family."

Manuel's eyes narrowed. "That sounds like my mom. My dad would fall apart without her—she does everything. My dad thinks he's the boss, but it's really my mom."

"My mom's all alone," Juan admitted. "But I'm glad Dad left because he used to mouth off to her all the time."

"Sounds like my dad," Charlie said, cracking his knuckles. "When he's drunk, all he does is bad mouth my mom. That's when I can't take it and I get the hell out."

"Why doesn't she kick him out?" Manuel asked, his voice incredulous.

"That's what I used to think," Juan explained. "But it isn't that easy. Mom could never kick Dad out."

Moses took a deep breath. "My mom's been taking care of our family ever since Dad went to prison. Guess I never really thought about her being strong and powerful."

"To be a noble man," I explained in a firm, steady voice, "we need to respect all women, even the girls at school, treat them with the same honesty and respect as we do our mothers."

"Who says I respect my mother?" Charlie interrupted.

"Who *do* you respect?" Manuel asked in a sarcastic tone.

"My friends, that's who."

Before things could get completely out of hand, I decided to bring the discussion back to my own life experiences.

"The first person to honor and respect is yourself. When I was a teenager, I felt as if I wasn't worth anything. I looked to my friends for what I didn't have at home or for what I couldn't find inside of myself. My mother tried to help, but she was too busy trying to survive. Many of my friends felt hopeless like I did."

"*Híjole,* Mr. G.," Manuel said. "So how *did* you make it?"

Pushing my chair back, I rose to my feet. "I had people who believed in me, who showed me I had value. That's why I'm here, to help you see that you do have value, that you are worthy. I'm here to show you that you can become *hombres nobles* like me."

The room suddenly grew quiet and gazing at their faces, I knew my words had made an impact on them.

TWENTY
Moses

I'm standing in front of my locker, thinking about how I am going to dread Thanksgiving at the prison, when Marissa's voice snaps me out of my mood.

"Hey, Moses. Are you coming to the MEChA meeting?"

Before I can answer, Manuel comes strolling up to her side. "Don't you worry," he tells her. "We'll both be there."

"I wasn't talking to you, *estúpido*," Marissa says, smacking him on the arm before she races away with her friend, who is laughing hysterically.

I shake my head at Manuel, wondering how I ever agreed to go with him to the meeting. "Don't you ever get tired of acting like some kind of macho man?"

"No way, bro," Manuel says, a conceited smile on his face that reminds me of Arturo.

By the time we walk into the multi-purpose room, the MEChA meeting has already begun. We take the two empty seats behind Julie just as Micaela signals for Mr. G., who's now standing next to Marissa.

"And now, Mr. Gutiérrez has some important news to share."

"Last week, I delivered the clothes that you collected to Friendly Helpers. They asked me to let all the club members know how grateful they were for the donation. They also said to keep the clothes coming."

I'm determined not to react, reminding myself that it's not about me. My mind wanders to that day at Tehachapi, when the guards wouldn't let two *viejitos* with their grandkids visit with their son because they were wearing the wrong clothes. I'll never forget the old lady's tears as they turned around to leave.

Leaning forward in my chair, I whisper to Julie, "That was a nice idea you had."

When Julie turns around and thanks me, the nervousness in my stomach slowly fades away. I look back up to the front of the room as Micaela thanks Mr. G.

"That's great," she tells him. "I'm so happy our club is able to do something like that." Taking a step closer to the small group gathered around her, Micaela raises her voice to say, "I have an important announcement. It's so sad, but Andrea will no longer be our treasurer." Then she turns to Andrea and gently asks, "Would you like to say a few words to the club members?"

Andrea lowers her eyes, caressing the Virgen de Guadalupe necklace hanging from the silver chain that she's wearing. "My family is moving to Sacramento. I hate it, but my dad got transferred to another AT&T plant."

Watching her wipe away a tear sliding down her left cheek, I'm reminded of all the times we've had to move. If anyone knows exactly how Andrea feels having to change schools and leave all their friends behind, it's me. Sometimes it hurts so bad, but there's nothing you can do to change anything.

"So it looks like we're going to need a new treasurer," Micaela says in a sad voice. "Are there any nominations?"

Manuel is suddenly on his feet. "I'd like to nominate Moses for treasurer. He's really good at math."

When Marissa and Zakiya second the nomination, Micaela looks directly into my eyes, "Well, Moses, what do you say?"

I can feel myself start to blush. My heart is beating wildly, like a car bomb ready to explode.

"Come on, Moses, say yes." Manuel insists, giving me a playful tap on the shoulder before he sits back down.

Unable to take the stares any longer, I nod at Micaela, mumbling a feeble "yes" as the room fills with cheers.

After lunch, I'm in a state of shock about being voted in as the new treasurer of MEChA. I can't help but feel excited about it, but I'm a little annoyed that Manuel didn't give me a heads up. It isn't until I'm in computer science and we're updating our blogs that I forget all about Manuel. There are already a bunch of comments in response to the introduction I posted. The first one reads: *My dad's in prison too. He's been there for most of my life, so I know how bad it feels. I cry a lot for my dad. I've always missed having him around.* It's signed, *Daddy's Little Girl.*

The next post is anonymous and it's a total contrast to the first one: *Who needs a Dad anyway? I've got my homies, that's all I need. Get strong bro.* But it's the last one that really gets to me: *Dude, I'm with you. I lie all the time about my dad. Sometimes I tell people he's in the military, other times I say my parents are divorced. It's become like a game for me. Yours truly, The Great Pretender.*

I sit there and wonder what I can possibly reply to The Great Pretender or to any of them for that matter, when Mrs. Stern is suddenly at my table.

"Moses, how is your blog coming along?"

"It's good. I've already received some comments."

"I'm not surprised; your blog is very original. We're having a workshop next semester to discuss the use of technology in the classroom and I'll be talking about student blogs. I'd like to feature yours. I wouldn't use your name. It would be anonymous."

I can feel my head spinning from all the familiar doubts and fears. Just as I'm about to say no, I remember what Mr. G. said in our last Círculo, that to be *un hombre noble*, we need to recognize our own value. "Sure, that would be cool," I answer. Mrs. Stern gives me a thumbs up.

∽ ∽ ∽

We're at the dinner table, when I break the exciting news to Mom.

"Something good happened at school."

Mom glances up at me from the *pico de gallo* that she's piling on her meatloaf. "And what was that?"

"I was elected as the new treasurer of the MEChA Club."

"*M'ijo*, I'm so proud of you," Mom says. She gets up from the table to give me a hug. "Wait until your dad hears the news."

That's all it takes for Carmen to begin to wiggle in her seat as if she has to go to the bathroom. "I can't wait to see

Daddy tomorrow!" she shouts. "I'm going to wear my new blouse with the happy faces!"

Smiling, Mom says, "*Hijo*, your dad will be so proud of you when he finds out."

For once, I don't argue with Mom or say anything bad about Dad.

TWENTY-ONE
Moses

It only takes a half hour to be processed at the prison this morning since we're numbers ten, eleven and twelve. Maybe I'm imagining it, but the guards seem more relaxed. I could hardly believe it when they let a little kid pass through inspection even though he was wearing a sweatshirt with a hood. Guess they realized he couldn't possibly be a gang member.

The visiting room doesn't seem as bleak today. There are cardboard turkeys with smiling pilgrims pasted on the walls and on the vending machines. We even get to sit at a corner table near the back patio door, which is a good spot because every time an officer opens the door, we get a whiff of fresh air.

The moment mom's prison friend, Rosie, arrives she and Carmen go over to her table, leaving me alone to look around. When an officer comes down the aisle escorting a handcuffed prisoner toward the small visiting booths directly behind our table, I remember the time I asked Dad why those men couldn't visit with the rest of us. Dad explained that the small visiting booths were for the inmates who were in the "hole," solitary confinement. Then he told Mom that some men were in the hole for months, even years. Back then, I didn't think twice about it, but now I can't imagine being locked up alone for days, months, even years.

When I glance toward the front, Mom, Dad and Carmen are walking up to our table holding hands.

"Happy Thanksgiving, *hijo*," Dad says, as they sit down. "Güero lent me one of his new shirts for today."

I stare at his blue prison shirt, wondering how long it took him to make those perfect creases on the sleeves.

Pointing to his black shoes, Dad tells Mom, "See how shiny they are, *vieja*? I worked on them all night just for you."

Mom smiles back at him like a lovesick teenage girl. Then Carmen sticks out her feet so that Dad can admire her white boots. "Mine are shiny too!" she brags.

"Yes, they are," Dad agrees, squeezing her little hand as he and Mom exchange another smile.

The next thing I know Mom says, "Moses is an officer of a club. And he has a new computer too."

And before she says anything else, Carmen begins to do the pee dance. Mom stands up, grabbing Carmen by the hand.

"Go ahead, *hijo*. Tell your Dad about it while we go to the bathroom."

Hesitating, I describe the MEChA meeting to Dad and how I was voted in as the new treasurer. "My friend, Manuel, was the one who nominated me."

"Movimiento Estudiantil Chicano de Aztlán," Dad repeats, his dark brown eyes shining. "I'm very proud of you, Moses."

The words feel stuck in my throat. All these years, I thought Dad was stupid.

"How do you know what the acronym stands for?" I ask him.

"I read about it, in a Chicano history book I checked out from the library."

For a second, I want to tell him about my new blog, but instead, I tell him about the refurbished computer Mrs. Harrison gave me.

Dad surprises me one more time when he says, "In one of my GED classes, we studied basic computer technology. I'm hoping to apply for an office job, so I can get out of the paint department." His voice suddenly grows hoarse. "*Hijo*, when I come home, we're going to spend a lot of time together. You can teach me everything you know about computers."

Then he bows his head, staring at the empty Styrofoam cup in front of him. After a long moment of silence, he lifts his head, tears filling his eyes. "*My* dad was a bad drunk— used to beat me all the time. I could never do anything right for him. I've never told this to anyone before, not even to your mom. Your grandma always knew, but she never wanted to talk about it. He left us for good when I was around your age. Moses, I promise you, it won't be like that for us."

Before I can process Dad's startling confession, Carmen and Mom return to our table. "Daddy, I'm starving," Carmen says, pulling at his arm.

I can feel the tension in my body begin to ease as we rise from the table and head for the vending machines. It's not until after we've eaten and I'm all alone at the table that

I'm able to sort out my emotions. I never knew Dad suffered that way.

I think about Charlie and Juan, the way they talked about their Dads in the Círculos. I'm deep in thought when I feel someone tap me on the shoulder. I turn around to find Dalana and her parents standing behind me.

"Happy Thanksgiving," Dalana says. "We're leaving now, but I wanted you to meet my parents."

Standing up, I shake hands with Dalana's mother, who has the same beautiful eyes and dark brown skin. Then I shake hands with Mr. Coleman, who is several inches taller than me.

"Where are your parents?" Dalana asks. "I wanted to meet them."

"They took my little sister for a walk on the front patio."

"It's nice to meet one of my daughter's friends from school," Mr. Coleman says. "What quad is your father in?"

"I'm not sure," I answer, wondering if he thinks I'm an idiot for not knowing.

"Tell your dad I'm in C-Quad. Maybe he can come by sometime."

As they turn around to leave, Dalana leans into me, whispering, "I'm so glad you decided to come see your dad."

When visiting hours come to an end, we wait until we hear the final warning before we rise from the table. The guards are anxiously rushing everyone out the door, so Dad only has time to give each of us a quick hug.

"Thanks, son. Thanks for coming to see me," Dad hollers out, as he hurries to line up against the wall with all the other inmates.

Waving back at him, I feel a huge lump in my throat as I follow Mom and Carmen out the thick prison door.

∾ ∾ ∾

Back in my bedroom that evening, I open up my computer, feeling compelled to write something on my blog: *I went to visit my dad for Thanksgiving at the prison today. I didn't want to go, but now I'm really glad I did because today my dad trusted me enough to tell me the truth about him and his dad. And for the first time I was able to understand him, to see him as a real person. I always thought he was a loser, not worth my time. I never realized how much he suffered growing up with an abusive father. My friend Dalana spoke the truth. Just because our dads are in prison, doesn't mean they're losers. Today I felt proud of my dad for the very first time.*

TWENTY-TWO
Ray Gutiérrez

I wondered how many of the boys would attend the Círculo today. It was always difficult for students to return to their regular classroom schedules after a holiday break. I found Moses sitting on the steps reading from a thick, gold book that resembled an encyclopedia.

"Interesting book?" I asked, unlocking the door to the multicultural center.

"Yeah, it is," Moses replied, placing it carefully inside his backpack and following me inside. "It smells like a dead animal in here."

"Why don't you open some windows while I re-arrange the chairs?"

Moments later, Juan Díaz walked into the room with Charlie right behind him.

"Perfect timing," I said. "As soon as Manuel gets here, we can get started."

"He's not coming," Moses spoke up. "He had to go to the dentist with his Mom."

As I sat down at the center of the group, I heard Juan mumble, "Lucky guy," but I ignored him.

"In that case, we'll go ahead and begin with our affirmations." I was completely surprised when each of the boys had something to say without me forcing it out of them. It was obvious they had been thinking about this during the holiday. After I thanked them for their affirmations, I turned to Charlie, who was on my left side.

"Would you like to share something about your Thanksgiving break?"

Leaning forward in his seat, Charlie raised his voice above the hum of the heater.

"Yeah, like my dad's a total fake. He actually sobered up, told mom he's quitting that he wanted us to be one big happy family for Thanksgiving. But he's not fooling me."

"Why don't you give your dad a break?" Moses asked.

"Oh, yeah? Look who's talking? Wish my dad were locked up."

Moses kept his voice steady. "You don't know what you're talking about. I saw my dad on Thursday and he told me how much he suffered when he was growing up. I found out my dad's not so bad after all."

"Hope is a wonderful thing," Charlie said in a sarcastic tone, tucking several strands of hair behind his left ear.

Juan shook his head fiercely, glaring at Charlie. "Dude, why do you have to act like that? Not everyone thinks like you. My uncle Sammy used to get in trouble a lot and now, he's doing some good things with his life."

"Would you like to tell us about your uncle?" I asked, hoping to bring some positive energy back into the room.

Nodding, Juan's voice softened. "We spent Thanksgiving in Fresno at my grandma's. My uncle Sammy was there. He's a teacher at the middle school and he coaches the basketball team, so we went to one of his games. It was cool seeing how all those kids look up to him." Turning to glare at Charlie again, Juan said, "My uncle said I could get a college degree, too, if I want."

"Not me," Charlie interrupted, shaking his head fiercely. "I'm gonna travel around the world, get as far away as I can from my old man."

"Is that right?" Moses asked. "It takes a lot of money to travel. How are you going to do that?"

"I'm gonna get a good job, make some good money, that's how."

Moses laughed. "Oh, yeah, minimum wage will buy you a whole lot of airplane tickets."

Charlie's face turned red and for a second, I thought he was going to hurl his skateboard at Moses.

"I certainly wouldn't be a counselor at Roosevelt if I hadn't obtained my university degree," I quickly spoke up. "Education opens doors for you. It empowers you."

"But not everyone's smart like you, Mr. G.," Juan admitted.

"It's all about *ganas*—believing in yourself."

"Screw that," Charlie said, slouching down in his chair. "All I need are my friends."

"And you think they're gonna fix your screwed up life?" Juan asked in an accusing tone.

Before Charlie could reply, Juan pleaded with me again. "Mr. G., do you really think I could be somebody like my uncle Sammy?"

"Of course you can," I nodded. "Look at me, I could've ended up in prison or maybe dead from gangbanging, but I didn't. That's why I'm here, to help you figure things out."

"Mr. G. is right," Moses agreed. "I always felt embarrassed about my dad being in prison. I thought I was all alone. But then I started this blog and found out there's a bunch of guys like me whose dads are in prison."

"Oh, so now you're this bleeding heart," Charlie hissed, cracking his knuckles. "Who the hell needs a father anyway?"

Moses' words were bold. "Me, that's who. I saw my dad cry for the first time when he told me how my grandpa used to beat him. He said that's why he always wants us to be close."

I recognized the important breakthrough that had just occurred for Moses. "It sounds like your dad was being very sincere about always being there for you. "

"I never really felt that until now," Moses agreed. "And I'm really glad Mom stuck by him all these years."

Charlie abruptly stood up, tucking his skateboard under his arm. "Have to go meet my friends," he mumbled as he headed toward the door.

I reluctantly called the meeting to an end. As I was gathering up my belongings, I heard Moses offer to help Juan with his math homework. I couldn't help but smile to myself, knowing that the Círculos were finally having a positive influence in their lives.

∽ ∽ ∽

Later that evening, I was in the living room watching the ten o'clock news, when my cell phone rang. I felt my heart take a giant leap when I heard David's voice on the other line.

"Hey, Dad—I've only got a minute. My game was cancelled next weekend, so I was thinking maybe I would come visit."

"Of course, son. I'd love that."

"Okay, see you."

At that, I heard an abrupt click. Taking a long, deep breath, my thoughts turned to Moses and his father. Yes, it was all about forgiveness.

GLOSSARY

Ándale, hijo. Es su cumpleaños—Come on, son. It's his birthday.

Apá—father; abbreviation for papá.

Aquel malvado dictador—That evil dictator.

Ay, m'ijo—Oh, my son.

carne asada—grilled beef.

chisme—gossip.

chismelandia—Chicano Spanish word that combines the Spanish word, "chisme" or gossip with the English word "land." or landia.

chile con carne—chili beans.

chismosas—gossipy persons.

chula(s)—cute; pretty.

Círculo(s)—small gatherings or group sessions based on the Círculos de Hombres Nobles that were developed as a vital component of the National Compadres Network.

comadre/compadre—a female/male protector; close family friend; a relative of mutual consent, which may not be by blood.

comal—hot plate for cooking tortillas.

¿Cómo estás, hijo?—How are you, son?

compadre—a male protector; close family friend; a relative of mutual consent, which may not be by blood.

corrido—a ballad or song that was popularized during the Mexican Revolution.

cumbia(s)—a type of dance music of Columbian origin similar to salsa.

El Pueblo de Nuestra Señora La Reina de Los Ángeles— the original name of Los Angeles (the Town of Our Lady, the Queen of Los Angeles) dating back to 1781.

Es buena gente—He's a good person.

estúpido—stupid.

familia—family.

ganas—desire or a wish to accomplish something.

guayabera—traditional shirt worn in Mexico or Latin America.

hijo—son.

¡Híjole!—Wow!; My goodness!; Oh my gosh!

güero—a light-skinned or fair-haired person.

indio(s)—Indigenous people.

jefito/a—parent or head of family male or female.

La Palabra—being a man of your word; concept from the National Compadres Network.

Lucha libre—refers to all forms of professional wrestling in Spanish-speaking areas.

Male Voices Project—a National Organization to empower young males.

más gente—more polite or kind.

MEChA—Movimiento Estudiantil Chicano de Aztlán; an early student organization that was formed during the Chicano Civil Rights Struggle of the 1960s.

m'ijita/o—the contraction of "my little daughter/son."

milagro—a miracle.

National Compadres Network—a National Organization co-founded in 1988 by internationally known speaker and activist, Jerry Tello, to address a variety of issues affecting marginalized youth and their communities such as gang violence and teen fatherhood.

norteña(s)—regional Tex-Mex music that encompasses regional ensembles and their particular styles.

¡Órale!—Hey!; Okay!; All right!

padrecito—little priest; an endearment.

panadería—bakery.

pendejo—idiot; fool; a stupid person.

¡Qué bueno!—That's good.

¿Qué es eso de refurbished?—What does that mean, refurbished?

¿Qué no?—Is that right?

rancheras—a genre of traditional Mexican music played by Norteño or Banda groups.

Raza—race, lineage, family. La raza is a concept that includes all Latinos regardless of nationality.

Se puso como loca—She went crazy; she lost it.

tamales—a traditional Mexican dish of indigenous origin made with meat or other ingredients wrapped in corn husks.

taquería—a Mexican restaurant that specializes in tacos and burritos.

telenovelas—Spanish soap operas.

tonto—dummy.

trucha—Watch out.

Un Hombre Noble—Noble Man; a concept from the National Compadres Network.

vagos—bums.

vato—dude; homeboy.

veteranos—common term used in reference to former gang members.

viejitas/os—little old ladies; little old men.

Virgen de Guadalupe—Mexico's most honored patron saint, the brown Virgin Mary.

Also in the Roosevelt High School Series

Ankiza

Juanita Fights the School Board

Maya's Divided World

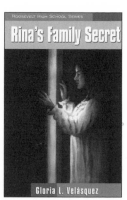

Rina's Family Secret

Also in the Roosevelt High School Series

Rudy's Memory Walk

Teen Angel

Tommy Stands Alone

Tommy Stands Tall

Tyrone's Betrayal

Gloria L. Velásquez created the Roosevelt High School Series "so that young adults of different ethnic backgrounds would find themselves visible instead of invisible. When I was growing up, there weren't any books with characters with whom I could relate, characters that looked or talked like Maya, Juanita or Ankiza. The Roosevelt High School Series [RHS] is my way of promoting cultural diversity as well as providing a forum for young people to discuss serious issues that impact their lives. I often will refer to the RHS Series as my 'Rainbow Series' since I modeled it after Jesse Jackson's concept of the rainbow coalition."

Velásquez has received numerous honors for her writing and achievements, such as being featured for Hispanic Heritage Month on KTLA, Channel 5, Los Angeles, an inclusion in *Who's Who Among Hispanic Americans*, *Something About the Author* and *Contemporary Authors*. In 1989, Velásquez became the first Chicana to be inducted into the University of Northern Colorado's Hall of Fame. The 2003 anthology, *Latina and Latino Voices in Literature for Teenagers* and *Children*, devotes a chapter to Velásquez's life and development as a writer. Velásquez is also featured in the 2006 PBS Documentary, *La Raza de Colorado*. In 2007, she was also included in the award-winning anthology *A-Z Latino Writers and Journalists*. In 2004, Velásquez was featured in "100 History Making Ethnic Women" by Sherry Park (Linworth Publishing). Stanford University recently honored her with "The Gloria Velásquez Papers," archiving her life as a writer and humanitarian.